CLAIMED

POWERTOOLS: THE SHIELDS, BOOK 5

JAYNE RYLON

HAPPY ENDINGS PUBLISHING

V3

eBook ISBN: 978-1-947093-33-1

Print ISBN: 978-1-947093-34-8

Cover Design by Jayne Rylon

Editing by Mackenzie Walton

Proofreading by Fedora Chen

Formatting by Jayne Rylon

ABOUT THE BOOK

Sometimes love is messy. Especially if three shattered souls are involved.

When Karolena answered an ad for a live-in housekeeper responsible for taking care of at least a dozen guys, she was obviously desperate.

Although she hadn't realized they were spies and assassins when she accepted the position, it could work out for the best since the Shields' headquarters might be the only place she's safe from the evil ex hunting her.

That is, if she doesn't give in to the two agents that live across the hall who tempt her to do things that could be dangerous to her still healing heart.

Tavish is more than willing to show Karolena a good time so long as that's as far as it goes. He's learned the very hard way that it's fine to sleep with women, or men, so long as you don't trust them.

That's only becasue Tavish's partner—both in the field and the bedroom—has always made sure his judgement isn't compromised when they surrender to their non-traditional urges together. Legend is the one person

Tavish is certain has his back since he's proved it over and over on life or death missions yet still, he's not able to give the man the affection he deserves along with plenty of satisfaction.

So when they find themselves entangled with their housekeeper, and her ties to the mafia, they have to decide whether she's capable of bringing the three of them together permanently or whether they have to get rid of her before she wrecks them for good.

From New York Times and USA Today bestselling author Jayne Rylon comes a steamy new multi-partner series of interconnected standalones set in the Powertools universe.

ADDITIONAL INFORMATION

Sign up for the Naughty News for contests, release updates, news, appearance information, sneak peek excerpts, reading-themed apparel deals, and more. www.jaynerylon.com/newsletter

Shop for autographed books, reading-themed apparel, goodies, and more www.jaynerylon.com/shop

A complete list of Jayne's books can be found at www.jaynerylon.com/books

ACKNOWLEDGMENTS

Thanks to Kelley Hopkins, whose suggestion for how to torture James and his car received the most votes in the poll in my Rylon Readers Facebook group :)

Join us there for fun stuff like this!

1

K arolena should have considered how much she hated getting her hands dirty before she'd accepted a job as a glorified maid for an entire building full of dangerous men and women. Especially since her new co-workers reminded her so much of the bad people she was running from.

Except even in the twenty-four hours she'd been employed by Shields Security Services, she could see its staff members weren't precisely the same as her evil ex. Or maybe she simply wanted to believe she hadn't landed herself in worse trouble than the sort she'd so recently, *hopefully* escaped.

She prayed again that she'd spent enough time around liars and thieves to have faked her background check well enough to pass the scrutiny of her new bosses.

Karolena wrenched the cap off a fresh bottle of cleaner, breaking yet another nail in the process. Of course. As she dumped the hyper-blue liquid into the bucket at her feet, each glug of chemicals did nothing to cheer her mood. Her mop plopped into the mixture with enough force to slosh a fountain of now-sudsy water onto the slate tiles of the kitchen floor she was attempting to make shine. If only she'd ever done routine housework before, she might have better technique.

Was getting it so wet going to mess up the grout or wreck the finish? She had no clue.

Karolena groaned. She couldn't afford to lose this job. As shitty as the work was, the opportunity had met every requirement of her desperate plan. It paid better than anything else she'd seen given she had exactly zero skills or qualifications. It also came with room and board. Even benefits. Plus a bonus she hadn't even hoped for...built-in security. Because although the Shields didn't realize she was on the run, they sure as hell weren't about to let random strangers wander into their headquarters.

Especially not when they and their loved ones, including the founder Jordan's pregnant wife, lived there too. Karolena had lucked into the perfect haven and she couldn't fuck it up now.

"Wow, that's really foaming up."

Karolena jolted.

How was Tavish so quiet in those black leather boots that paired so nicely with his kilt? She'd assumed the security guard—or whatever his actual title was—had been dressed up for the Shields' party the night before. If instead he planned on flashing those sexy legs covered in amber fur all the time, she was going to have to build an immunity to him, his cut muscles, and his easygoing appeal. His Scottish accent agitated her because it piqued her interest. It also reassured her given that her Russian heritage colored her own speech more than she'd like, even when she concentrated on stifling all hints of her foreign roots. No one here seemed to judge her for how she spoke or where she came from. For a company outside of a major metropolis, they seemed pretty accepting of people from way, way out of town.

Of course, they wouldn't be so nice if they knew who she really was and what she'd been a part of, unwitting or not.

Karolena forced herself to concentrate on the giant mess she was making before she gave herself more to clean. She swallowed hard. Even the astringent chemicals she'd probably used way too much of in the wash water couldn't completely obscure the scent of Tavish's soap or cologne or whatever that spicy vanilla smell was that she was quickly beginning to associate with him.

He leaned in for a closer look, his slightly longer than shoulder-length hair tumbling forward over his collarbones. Tavish scooped the locks into one hand and pulled them into some messy half-up, half-down topknot, man-bun thing that she never would have expected to find attractive. Yet on him, it was.

"Is it supposed to do that?" Tavish pointed at the foam expanding across his floor. The mat of bubbles thickened until it looked as if winter had come early. The apartment he shared with his partner, Legend, gave off upscale rustic vibes, grounded in comfort. Weathered wood, stone, and wrought iron details came together beautifully. It made her feel like she'd been safely ensconced in a bear den. Or maybe it was the size and dark scruff of Tavish's roommate that gave her that impression. Karolena shivered even as she hoped she didn't ruin anything in their home.

To distract herself, she took the mop and flailed around in the lather with it. That only made it expand faster, gobbling up her ankles and the mat in front of the sink. Tavish hopped back to spare his boots. Maybe this wasn't how it was supposed to go?

How the hell would she know if the floor cleanser was working properly? Oh, right. She was supposed to be a professional.

She hated to admit it, but seeing her nails already ragged and uneven instead of perfectly manicured didn't improve her mood. When had she become used to being pampered? Was that why it had taken her so long to break away from Vladimir despite the way he'd treated her for years?

Karolena attempted to disperse the ridiculous pile of suds along with her dark thoughts by smooshing them around with enough force that the mop handle creaked. Her frantic swipes only seemed to agitate the soap, increasing its volume instead of reducing it. Sort of like the feelings that kept bubbling up inside her now that she was, for the moment, safe.

"Everything okay in here?" Legend asked as he passed through the kitchen, hopping from the edge of her multiplying disaster then over it entirely like an elegant and considerate socked gazelle instead of the grizzly he resembled.

"It's fine." She intended to talk to Tavish, Legend, and the rest of the Shields as little as possible. If they would go away she could get the situation under control without their watchful stares on her every movement.

These men and the rest of their friends were capable and insightful. She would be foolish to forget it.

Not only because of the predatory movements they made or the way their eyes stalked her as she worked near them. Not only because of the gun safes she'd spotted tucked neatly into each of their closets when she was wrestling with the vacuum earlier. Not only because she'd explicitly and repeatedly been warned that the basement was strictly off limits. Not only because they might figure out where she'd come from and either kick her out or send her back.

But also because they could so easily make her care. Something she'd sworn never to do again. James with his quirky fashion, tact, and conversational interview style had thawed the first corner of her heart. Kennedy, who'd reviewed their medical benefits including mental health services and asked if there was anything Karolena needed right away had cracked her resolve to be cold and aloof. The endless parade of laughing, ridiculously happy lovers Tavish had introduced her to the night before made her wish for a fairytale ending of her own.

It was a temptation she had to resist.

While avoiding Tavish and Legend's curious stares, Karolena glanced at the photograph magneted to the side of the refrigerator she was swiping around in an attempt to spread out the mountain of bubbles. Of Tavish, in a more formal kilt. Craggy mountains pierced a bright blue sky in front of a still, deep lake. Boulders tumbled around the edges were blanketed in green and yellow moss. It made a dramatic backdrop for the bridal party he had been part of. Off to the side of the groom, who looked too much like him to be anything other than a brother—or a maybe a cousin—Tavish cheered as the happy couple kissed.

Did moments like that happen in real life? At least for some people?

Something so ordinary and beautiful and traditional seemed far more improbable to her than the life she'd lived, which would probably seem out of reach to most.

Sure, it had been filled with luxury and glitz, endless wealth and a ruthless pursuit of more, but it hadn't meant anything to her.

None of it had been real.

And all of it had come at the expense of so many innocents.

Karolena shuddered. She hadn't been a willing participant in the crimes that had funded her crystalline prison, but she had seen plenty and been helpless to stop it for long enough that it would haunt her for the rest of her life. Especially if she managed to break free when so many others hadn't been so lucky.

"Hey, don't freak out." Tavish must have misunderstood the cause of her deep introspection. "This is no problem. Let me help you—"

"No, thank you. I've got it under control." Karolena didn't even believe her own lie. Frantically, she resumed trying to snuff out the ever-expanding white blob now engulfing half the kitchen. "Or I will. Just give me a minute. Please."

She took a deep breath through chattering teeth, memories still assaulting her.

"Cold?" Legend asked, proving he hadn't wandered far from his partner or the intruder in their private space. He obviously hadn't missed her visceral reaction to her memories either. She was going to have to rely more heavily on the masking skills she'd developed during her time with Vladimir. "I can set the AC to something more reasonable. I turned it down earlier so you wouldn't get sweaty while working. I hate when that happens to me."

"You're hot even when you're doing nothing." Tavish's breath hitched, causing Karolena's stare to wing between the two men now bookending her. Was there something between the partners beyond their professional bond?

And why did being in such close proximity to them, alone, do anything but freak her out like it should? Especially since Tavish had been less than subtle with his come-ons from the moment he'd held the front door open for her before her interview and then been assigned to show her around once she'd accepted the position and moved in right next door the night before.

When Tavish swallowed hard and flicked an imaginary piece of lint from the hem of his kilt, she shook her head and returned to dispersing as many of the suds as she could.

"The temperature's fine. I mean, good. It's great. That was thoughtful. Thank you." Why the hell was everyone being so nice to her? Vladimir wouldn't so much as notice the help, never mind change the thermostat to make them more comfortable.

Karolena's gaze wandered one last time to the photograph on the refrigerator as she shoveled some foam onto the mop and attempted to drown it in the bucket. Tavish obviously had a family and friends he loved and who loved him too. What was he doing here, on the other side of the world from them? If she'd had a choice, she never would have left hers.

Her father, circumstances, and Vladimir had stolen that option from her years ago.

Any warm feelings she'd been harboring evaporated in an instant. Anyone who could abandon their loved ones didn't deserve her lusting for them. And certainly didn't warrant a chink in her armor for their basic decent gestures.

She would never allow herself to be blinded to someone's true nature so easily again.

Lucky for Karolena, she wasn't a naïve sixteen-year-old girl anymore. She'd seen enough shit in her decade of...imprisonment? Display? Whatever she'd call her time with Vladimir. Which was certainly not *a marriage* despite their very public and elaborate ceremony.

"How much of this did you use?" Legend wondered, reading the back of the bottle she'd set on the counter.

"The whole thing, obviously," she muttered as she glared at the empty vessel. She wasn't about to skimp. If they wanted her to clean, she was going to make the place gleam.

Tavish cracked up, clutching his lean abdomen. All she could think of for a moment were the ripped abs he'd flashed when changing his shirt while she was dusting earlier. She blinked at him.

"It's concentrate, Karolena." Legend drew her attention back to his frowning face. "The instructions say you only need a capful for every three gallons of water."

Hadn't the sticker on the side of the bucket said it only held two? Damn it.

"Sorry. I'm used to liters, not gallons." How pissed would he be if she'd ruined their kitchen? Vladimir wouldn't have hesitated to fire her. Or worse. "I'll fix this. I promise."

Legend only smiled kindly. "James bought us each a set of extra-absorbent microfiber towels we use to cover the gym equipment. I'll go grab ours and we can sop this up."

Karolena shook her head. "Just tell me where they are and I'll do it. It's my mistake."

"We'll feel less weird about having you clean our mess

in the first place if you let us pitch in," Tavish argued. Legend nodded.

The fizzle of the rising bubbles cut through the silence that stretched between them. But before she could agree, a knock at the door startled her. She spun around so fast she knocked over the mop, the handle falling through the cloud of bubbles and bouncing noisily on the tiles of the submerged flooring, lost.

"It's okay." Tavish put his hand on her shoulder even as Legend stepped so that he stood between her and the entrance. No one was getting to her without going through him first.

Something uncurled inside Karolena that had been tightly wound since she darted into the night—alone and bleeding, on the outskirts of Saint Petersburg, as Levin watched her flee.

"There's nothing to be afraid of here," Tavish cooed to her, his brogue thicker as he did.

Not unless it was them. And the kindness so many strangers had already shown her.

"What are you three doing in there?" a woman singsonged from the other side of the entry. "You know I can hack the pinpads on all these doors, right?"

"Ruby." Legend growled. It was odd to see a man as big and...solid...as him roll his eyes. And yet his exasperation, reserved for their newcomer's little-sister energy, somehow put Karolena at ease.

Tavish grinned, then trudged through the bubbles to shove Legend's shoulder. "Let her in before she starts to think there's something a lot more fun than mopping going on in here. Unless you'd like to start moaning really loud and make her think we're as slick as she suspects."

Karolena barely choked down the laugh that threatened to emerge from her tight throat.

Shit. She hadn't even been there a full day and already she was letting these people erode the barriers she'd erected to keep herself safe.

She was officially fucked.

Restraining the urge to swat Tavish or lob a ball of suds at him for teasing her and Legend, Karolena went back to corralling the disaster instead of trying to pry as their co-worker entered.

"Boys, we need you downstairs for a meeting." Ruby flashed a smile at Karolena before her eyes went wide. "What the hell...?"

"Nothing. It's not a big deal." Tavish blocked her view of Karolena's catastrophe.

Grateful, she peeked up at him and the red-haired woman wearing a graphic tee with a cartoon character across her chest. Ruby engaged in some sort of silent communication with Legend that irrationally irked Karolena.

After a few moments Ruby tossed her loose braid over her shoulder, then smiled. Unfortunately, it didn't seem entirely genuine. "Anyway, boys, let's go. This shouldn't take too long."

"Must be important. Nothing good ever happens this early," Tavish grumbled. "Fine, we're coming."

"Do you want me to leave and finish this when you're here to...supervise?" Karolena gritted her teeth, but she would understand if they said yes. She was a stranger to them. They had no way of knowing they didn't have anything she coveted except for a way to earn her freedom.

"Nah. Do what you gotta do." Tavish waved his hands

in front of his chest. "Probably best to get this under control sooner rather than later. Those towels we were talking about are in the hall closet at eye-level. Sorry in advance for the state of Legend's bathroom when you make it that far."

Legend smacked Tavish in the gut with the back of his hand. "Quit that."

"Just kidding." Tavish winked at her. Despite her well-used bitch façade, Karolena felt herself cracking a bit of a smile at their antics. Especially when Tavish strode toward her then reached over, not too quickly, and wiped a daub of bubbles from her cheek with the pad of his thumb. The things his caress did to her should have terrified her more than Vladimir's brutality ever had.

When was the last time she'd felt at home? At peace? These men, and this place, might be even more dangerous than she'd realized at first.

Legend pointed to a spray bottle hanging on the cleaning cart James had supplied her with. "That one has bleach. You'll want to use it, in moderation, for the bathroom. But not on anything—like fabrics—where the color could leech out."

"Uh, right. Thanks." She winced, damn sure she'd read the directions before putting it on anything.

Before she could turn away, Tavish tucked a tendril of her platinum hair into the messy bun she'd wrangled it into as if passing the gesture along from his roommate. The layers meant wisps kept escaping. It wasn't a practical cut, but then again, she'd never considered having to put it up during a shift of manual labor.

This was her punishment. She'd lived a life of luxury at other people's expense. And now it was time to pay.

"Knock on the conference room door if you need anything," Legend said.

And then they were gone.

Karolena took a deep breath, shook her head to clear it, then got to work dispersing the mountain of suds. It was easier to breathe, and think straight, without Tavish and Legend screwing with her mind and parts farther south.

2

———

Legend puffed at the wad of suds on his forearm, launching them into the air. They split into smaller globules that careened into the walls and the floor, popping on contact. He shook his head and rounded on Tavish. "You can't pull that shit with Karolena."

Ruby's brows rose until they nearly disappeared in her hairline. Great, just what they needed. Over-interested friends involved in their relationships or lack thereof.

Tavish pretended not to feel the full force of his wrath, only shrugging. "Pull what?"

"Flirting with her like that. What were you going to do, fuck her on the kitchen counter?"

"Would have been more fun in all those bubbles, huh?" The corner of Tavish's mouth quirked up in a way that did nothing to deescalate the tension—sexual and otherwise—that sparked between them too damn easily.

"Tavish," Legend growled. The last thing they needed was to stroll into a meeting with boners.

Ruby snorted. When Legend included her in his

glower, she mimed zipping her lips and tossing the key over her shoulder. So he returned his ire to the person who deserved it.

"Don't harass her, asshole. She's just trying to do her job." Legend wasn't saying he didn't like the idea of getting wet and slippery with both Tavish and Karolena on the kitchen floor, but he was also man enough to recognize they hadn't met her at a bar or on some dating app. This was work. And worse, where they lived.

Hazards surrounded them like a tangle of tripwires. Risking blowing up something important in exchange for a couple of orgasms, even really good ones? No, thank you.

"So, yeah, about that..." Ruby shot them a glance out of the corner of her eyes. "You might want to reserve judgment about our housekeeper until you hear what our meeting's about."

"No. *Her*? What now?" Tavish looked like someone had promised him a puppy then reneged on the deal. Did he already care that much? Sure, Legend had noticed their instant attraction, but so what? He and Tavish had entertained plenty of women, and a man or two, for one-night stands. They had no shortage of partners who'd welcome their attention.

Their ride down in the elevator was a bit awkward with Tavish pinching the bridge of his nose as he studied the toes of his boots. Legend's mood sank along with the shiny box that carried them to the main floor. He didn't relish the idea of having to be the voice of reason in the face of Tavish's hormones, but he'd do whatever it took to keep his partner safe, whether in the field or in their bedrooms.

When Legend entered the command center, he was

greeted by more than a dozen familiar faces already gathered around the giant gleaming table. Ones that belonged to the people he considered his brothers and sisters. He would, and often did, trust them with his life and looked out for them as well as he could. Nolan—with his perfectly coiffed hair—sat next to Kennedy, Marcus, and Knox, who held hands as they joked with him. Their sniper, Aarav, gave nothing away as he sipped his tea and watched his boyfriend, Cash, who was sitting with one ass cheek on the table, dip down to kiss their girlfriend, Sola.

Was it any mystery why Tavish and Legend seemed obsessed with finding someone who could fit them as well? They were surrounded by blissful trios who had everything they'd never imagined was possible—loving, equal relationships between three people who balanced each other out and fulfilled all the non-traditional needs they had. Lucky bastards. Each of them.

Even Ruby. Their resident cybergeek perked up as she passed her lovers on her way to the computer station at the brains of the command center, dragging the fingertips of one hand over both Ace and Liam from shoulder to shoulder as she strode behind them. It was as if she couldn't bear not to touch them despite the wild time he'd heard them having when he'd made his unofficial rounds in the middle of the night.

That meant Karolena had probably gotten an earful too, since her apartment—Ruby's old one—shared a wall with their bedroom and was right across the hall from his own place. Figured.

Legend wondered if Karolena had realized Ruby was being spoiled by both men, who also were into each other, and what she'd thought of it if she had. He'd kick his own ass if he could. Hadn't he just told Tavish the woman was off limits?

At the head of the table, James and Jordan had their heads together, conversing. The air of triumphant celebration underlying the festivities the night before, which had commemorated an enormous payout to the firm from their last mission, had been replaced by caution and gravity.

Damn it. The break had been nice given the pressures of their positions.

What did this have to do with Karolena? Better they find out now before they spent any more time watching her flounder and fight to find her footing at Shields. Legend couldn't afford to like her in addition to lusting after her if there was something fishy about her sudden appearance in their world.

Shields meant too much to him to risk his career or his friends for a piece of ass, no matter how spectacular it was.

He glanced over at Tavish, who locked eyes with him. Unfortunately, Legend couldn't reassure the guy. Something was up.

"Everyone here?" Tavish cleared his throat. It was completely unlike him to hurry for anything, never mind to start what he usually called a boring-ass meeting.

James winged a glance in their direction, one perfectly manscaped brow arched and a smile on his glossed lips. "Got a date?"

"Never know." Tavish's smile split open, revealing bright white teeth that flashed against his pink-toned skin and the red of his facial hair. "Any reason why I shouldn't try for one?"

"Maybe." James's shoulders slumped. "Sorry."

"No maybe. Absolutely." Jordan's tone was a hell of a lot more steely. "The background check Karolena filled out...well, it doesn't check. At all."

"It's got more gaping holes than me after a birthday weekend with the Powertools," James grumbled.

"Dude." Nolan slicked a hand over his action-figure hair, then laughed at James. "I know we're close around here, but damn."

James's eyes twinkled. He wasn't a bit sorry.

Jordan was less easily distracted. "Honestly, James, didn't you even pass this application by Ruby before interviewing Karolena?"

"I did." James shot Ruby a look then as if apologizing for possibly getting her in trouble. "And the fact that her references were fake as well as her previous address not existing...well, I could tell she needed help and I wanted to see what we could do. That's why I stuck her with Legend and Tavish until we could discuss further."

Jordan shook his head. "Despite our...informalities... around here, this *is* a business. A complicated and sometimes treacherous one. We can't take in strays. Especially when we don't know where they came from or why they're lying about pretty much everything they've told us."

"Hopefully not about her passion for cleaning up after these slobs?" James asked.

Tavish snorted. "Sorry, my guy. She can't tell her pert ass from a broomstick. I spent all morning trying not to rip the vacuum out of her hands so I could do it my damn self. It was painful to watch. And I wouldn't be surprised if you suddenly see a waterfall of foam pouring out our windows to the ground floor."

Nolan chuckled. "Sounds like the first time I did my own laundry and thought the container was single-use."

"It's exactly like that." Tavish winced. "I hope she doesn't tackle the dirty clothes while we're down here."

"She's trying her best." Legend felt the need to take up for Karolena. He'd seen the flash of panic in her eyes when she'd done a temperature check on their reactions to her screw up. She was used to being punished for minor infractions. Harshly. Of that, he was sure.

Tavish spun to face him, a slow smirk curving his lips. "I knew you liked her too."

What was not to appreciate? She reminded him of a princess or a prima ballerina in a maid's uniform. There was something very Cinderella-esque about her that made him want to be Prince Charming. It was a complex a lot of the Shields had. They were born, or had been forged, into protectors. Men and women willing to do extreme things to defend the innocent.

He belonged here for a reason.

Maybe Karolena was it.

Tavish nodded, then squeezed his forearm. They were in trouble.

"Guys, I'm with Jordan on this." Liam was extra cautious after having nearly lost Ace on a mission not so long ago and then suffered through Ruby getting kidnapped. Even Ruby, though she didn't speak up, twiddled with the end of her braid. "We've got our families here."

"I know it makes me biased, but with Wren expecting..." Jordan sighed. "I'm trying to be impartial, but a baby changes everything."

"Especially *your* baby." James patted Jordan's hand. He was no stranger to loss either. That poor kid. In addition to a whole pack of overprotective aunts and uncles, who sometimes also happened to kill very bad people, Wren's baby was going to have a badass father who was relentless in looking after them. Legend felt sorry way in advance for whoever would end up being their first date. Jordan knew more ways to unalive someone and make the body disappear than most government agencies.

"Okay, I see your point. Really." James turned from Jordan to Legend and Tavish. "But now that you've spent some time with her, what's your take? Is she spying on us for someone? Or is she in trouble?"

Legend glanced at Tavish, who deferred his judgment, waiting to see what Legend would say. That was odd. Of the two of them, Legend was usually the quiet one. He shrugged. "It's only been a few hours, but I don't get the sense that she's a plant or anything like that. She's completely unartful. Just like with that background check. If someone we needed to worry about was going to send an operative to infiltrate our headquarters, they'd do a way better job. Right?"

Tavish nodded vehemently. "She's not an agent. She's afraid, though."

"Of what?"

"Dunno yet." Tavish kicked back and folded his hands on his taut stomach. "But I'm happy to get closer to her and find out."

"They *like* her like her," Ruby blurted. "She's probably a good apple, right?"

"Let's hope she doesn't have any poisonous seeds or a rotten core." Jordan sighed.

Legend put his elbow on the table and dropped his head into his hand. This could get messy quick.

"See, that's my sense too." James leaned forward,

drumming his fingers on the table. "We said someone would have to be desperate to take this job. And she absolutely is. But why? A woman like her...I'd bet she hasn't worked a day in her life. She was perfectly comfortable parrying with me in her interview. Sharp yet tactful. The kill-you-with-kindness sort. Her nails and hair weren't flashy but...pedigreed. Does that make sense?"

"Yeah, I could totally picture her as someone's trophy wife." Kennedy nodded. "I don't mean that as a negative, just that she seemed really good at small talk and pleasantries when we went over her benefits. Her posture is a solid ten out of ten too. But she's less comfortable with making decisions and showing vulnerability. She hesitated over picking a plan. And when I suggested some mental health services, her walls went up so fast I'd have thought the Powertools crew was building them."

James chuckled at the mention of his best friends and lovers, who also happened to own Middletown's booming construction business.

"Hiding out from someone, obviously," Jordan mumbled, a crack in his resistance showing. None of them could refuse to assist when they spotted a damsel in distress. It was their kryptonite. Begrudgingly, he caved, "Let's find out who. Quickly."

"We all agree she's not faking that accent, right?" Ruby asked, and the group nodded. That's one thing that hadn't wavered. "The bit I sampled off the security camera came back as Russian with a Baltic influence. Okay, let me start with reverse image searches narrowed to that region and I'll let you know what I come up with."

"Until we understand what's going on here, you two

aren't to let her out of your sight." Jordan pointed at Legend, then waggled his finger between him and Tavish.

Legend knew he should have been annoyed but instead, something inside him awoke and stretched. He wasn't disappointed by the opportunity to spend more time getting to know Karolena. Ah, shit.

Tavish swiveled his chair so he faced Jordan point blank. "Hypothetically, would it be okay if we stayed so close to her that we slept with her?"

Legend slapped his forehead. "Tavish!"

"Don't act like you don't want to." His partner huffed. "That wasn't a tree-trunk in your shorts this morning."

"Could have fooled me." James peeked over the edge of the table in the directions of Legend's bulge. "It's gotta be a two by four at least."

"Hey. What am I, a slab of meat?" Legend scowled, hoping they'd get the point. "I'm not and neither is she. If you weren't so busy staring at her tits in her soapy top you would have noticed she's nervous around us too."

"Probably because she's lying through her teeth about why she came here in the first place, not because she's afraid of us in particular." Tavish grinned. "Intimacy could be a shortcut to getting answers. What do you say, Jordan?"

"As long as you're not pressuring her into sleeping with you by holding the job, or our protection, over her head as leverage or something skeevy like that..."

"You think I'd do that?" Tavish's chin tucked down as if the thought alone was distasteful. It was to Legend too. They'd never had to resort to blackmail to lure a woman into their bed.

Jordan shrugged. "I'm not a micromanager. Nor am I your dad."

"If you end up screwing around with her, you better make it good and don't pull any stupid shit." James crossed his arms. "If you scare her away, you'll be cleaning every inch of this place on your days off."

Tavish chuckled. "I hate to break it to you, James, but she's seriously a shit housekeeper. I hope you have a plan B."

3

———

Karolena dried her hands on a rag as she appraised the kitchen. Okay, so it had taken her five times as long as it should have even without the Great Bubble Debacle, but she thought she'd done a pretty terrific job of making everything sparkle. It turned out that obsessing about whether or not she was about to be discovered and fired was perfect motivation for cleaning. She hated to admit it, but her tasks had turned out to be kind of cathartic.

Burning off anxiety by turning her worries into motion and progress wasn't the worst way to settle herself. She could think of only one *or two* better methods...

Damn it, why did Legend and Tavish appeal to her so much? And what would they do if they realized she was practically drooling over them both? Was it simply because for most of her life she hadn't had a choice of who to be with that the first men she met, she craved? Or because the man she'd been sold to was such a ruthless bastard?

Compared to Vladimir, anyone would look good.

Okay, so then why hadn't she latched onto James or Jordan or any of the men she'd been introduced to the day before? Well, most of them were taken, sure, and she wasn't the kind of woman to poach someone else's partner.

Even though she'd hated Vladimir, it had still wounded her when he'd slept around. The first time and the thousands of times later, after she'd realized her life would be so much better if he found other women attractive enough to leave her alone entirely.

She'd never gotten that lucky. But neither had he been interested in monogamy.

Of course, that didn't seem popular among the Shields either. Karolena's eyes had practically popped out of her skull when James had pointed to the photos of his husband *and* his wife in his office during her interview. Then the stream of people in polyamorous relationships Tavish had introduced her to at the party the night before had made it clear James wasn't the only one in Middletown who took the saying *the more the merrier* to heart.

Did Tavish and Legend? Intuition screamed yes.

Karolena had caught several of the looks they'd exchanged, communicating silently. Familiarity could be a benefit of their partnership in the security firm, but really, did patrolling the mall or bodyguard duties for local celebrities at the county fair—or whatever it was they did in this sleepy Midwestern town—forge that kind of bond?

Doubtful. But she'd bet she knew what kind of intense experience might.

The sort that involved setting the sheets on fire with each other and a very lucky woman between them.

Karolena had only ever really enjoyed sex a few times,

in the early days of her relationship with Vladimir, before she'd discovered how he'd become so wealthy and powerful and fully comprehended the horrors she'd ultimately endure while at his side. In the very beginning, she'd been foolish, trying to make the best of a terrible situation, gullible enough to believe him when he said he'd offered her father what he needed in exchange for her hand in marriage because he'd cared and not because he was a selfish prick who only gave a shit about his own desires and the easiest way to fulfill them.

She'd quickly realized how stupid she'd been to put faith in a single word that came out of his lying mouth. That had been a long time ago. More than a decade.

In that time she'd learned that most people, men especially, didn't put any significance in a quick fuck. So maybe it was time to take what she'd seen so many others enjoy.

This was a new life, and a new her, after all. Maybe she could become the sort of woman who sought her own pleasure, made sure to score several orgasms strong enough to actually relax her, then walked away without entanglements. Powerful, confident, and beholden to no one.

Karolena snorted at that. It had been less than a week since she'd slipped through Vladimir's clutches and used the phony papers Levin had supplied to get to the United States. She'd intentionally picked a place she'd never heard of in the heart of the country, then taken a bus to her new home. Cash hadn't been too much of a problem in the short-term. She had an entire backpack full. Plenty to reserve a hotel room and buy a few days to hunt for work.

It had happened so fast it was dizzying.

And there she was, in the middle of a beautiful apartment owned by two smoking hot men, daydreaming that somehow they would act on whatever flickers of desire she'd imagined had sparked between them earlier. That she had actually discovered people who wanted her for herself and not for her ties to Vladimir.

She'd better be careful or soon she'd have as big a head as her ex.

Karolena had transformed herself from the crown princess of the Russian mafia into a simple maid. And as she looked around at her handiwork, she thought that might not be so bad after all. She packed her supplies onto the cart and was wheeling it toward the door when Tavish and Legend returned from their meeting.

She beamed. "I took care of the...situation. Does everything look okay?"

"Damn, Karolena." Tavish glanced over her shoulder. "The place looks great. Did you even clean the windows?"

"Yes. There was glass spray here. I promise I checked the directions first. It said it was fine to use even if there was tint to block the sun." Their view was glorious. It featured the town surrounding the Shields headquarters, which gave way to lush fields, then finally wooded mountains with lakes that dotted the foothills in the distance.

She hoped they wouldn't mind that she'd taken a few minutes to absorb the scenery through their floor-to-high-ceiling wall of glass. With the sun shining and her problems half a world away, Karolena had started to appreciate that her future might be equally as brilliant.

"Maybe James was right." Legend wasn't staring at the windows, though. He was looking at her.

"Excuse me?" Karolena had been able to brush off

Tavish's earlier flirtations, but the heated stare coming from the man in front of her made her certain she hadn't been imagining anything after all.

Some uncommon connection arced between the three of them. One that both intrigued and frightened her. Lucky for the guys, she was still high on her progress and the thought of the opportunities stretching out in front of her like that gorgeous landscape. Infinite.

"That fucker usually is." Tavish saved Legend from explaining or Karolena from speculating further. "He thinks we have a thing for you...because we do...and he encouraged us to spend more time together. The three of us."

Legend grumbled something under his breath. When he looked up, his rich brown eyes—flecked with greens and golds—emitted a potent stare that locked on her.

In that moment, she realized she was way out of her league. These were experienced, worldly men and she had been isolated and stifled for her entire adult existence.

Karolena should have shoved her cart in between them, then bolted out the door before things could go any further than innuendo or steamy looks. But in that moment, an exceedingly rare one for her, she didn't want to do the cautious thing. So when Tavish came up behind her and started rubbing her shoulders, she didn't yank away. Nor did she have to steel herself against his touch.

She would have thought her body would instinctively knot with dread as it did when Vladimir approached her. And yet, it didn't. How sad was it that she feared these two men she'd only just met far less than she had her own husband?

With very good reason.

Tavish nudged her hair out of the way and slid his hands closer to rub the base of her neck. "You're not used to this, are you?"

"Being touched by a stranger? No, not at all." Vladimir would have killed anyone who had dared.

"I was referring to putting in a hard day's work. It's probably hell on your body until you get used to it." Tavish pressed a spot that inspired a soft moan to slip from her lips.

The sound dilated Legend's pupils as he took a half-step closer and then another. Was he trying to fight the attraction drawing them together as she had thought she would, but no longer cared to?

"There's a hot tub in the gym. It works magic on sore muscles." Legend glanced down as if imagining her in a bathing suit. She didn't own one. Hell, maybe they wouldn't mind skinny-dipping instead.

"Whatever he's doing is pretty damn great too." Karolena practically purred as Tavish proved his come-ons were backed by real skills. How far was she going to let this go?

How far was he willing to take it?

Apparently, all the way. Tavish murmured near her ear, "I could do a much better job if you'd let me take your clothes off and lay you down somewhere soft."

"And if I said yes, is that where it would stop?"

"Only if you insisted." Tavish nuzzled the side of her face, and still she didn't pull away, or break her stare with Legend.

"And would you join us?" she asked him, point blank.

"If that's what you want. *Is* that what you want, Karolena?" Legend wondered. The way her name sounded rumbling through his broad chest made her shiver in Tavish's hold. There was no denying she craved what they were offering—a chance to be bold, to be brave, and to be a little bit selfish by hoarding two men for herself.

Was it fast? Yes. Was either of them trying to twist her arm or hide their intentions? Not at all.

Somehow that reassured Karolena.

Wasn't the point of all this to gain her independence? Shouldn't that include the freedom to sleep with whomever she wanted for a night or more and enjoy every moment she could of the life she'd suffered so long to make her own?

Karolena's rational side knew it was a horrible idea, but the parts of her that had been caged, dormant and hopeless, were ready to be unleashed. If only for one impulsive fling.

"What would you do if I actually said yes to something that rash and ridiculous?" She crossed her arms to hide her hardening nipples from Legend.

He smiled, wide and slow. "I'd make it worth it. For all three of us."

"Oh."

Tavish chuckled. "He's not bragging either. It'll be an experience you never forget."

Could it also be one strong enough to erase some of her bad memories from past encounters? If there was even a tiny sliver of a chance that could be true, she was going to take it.

Legend might have been testing her. But if so, she called his bluff.

Why? Because she could if she chose to and she hadn't had that opportunity...well, ever.

Karolena had sacrificed everything for her autonomy.

If that meant seizing a chance to screw the man who had the sexiest pair of legs this side of the Atlantic and his mountain of a partner before her deranged ex-husband found her and either killed her or forced her to return to a living hell, she was going to take it.

"Okay, fine. Let's fuck."

4

———

Karolena tried not to grimace when Tavish's caresses faltered. He inhaled sharply. Had he expected Karolena to resist more? To be shy about her desires? Or was he as eager to get on with it as she was?

Either way, Legend was the voice of reason. Maybe in all things the partners did. "Make no mistake, I want this too. But tell us straight up. Should we be careful around you or do you need us to protect you?"

"Are you talking about using condoms?" Karolena tipped her head, arousal hazing her logic.

Tavish's rich laughter broke out. "He wasn't, but don't worry, we've got those and use them every time."

"Ah." Of course they did. They played by the rules. Unlike her ex. And that was one reason she felt comfortable enough to even consider something so outrageous.

Rational thought dissipated the more Tavish touched her, but something in Legend's warm eyes urged her to clarify. It was important to him. And so it should be to her if they were about to be intimate, if only for an afternoon quickie. "What *did* you mean?"

"I have a feeling you're here for a reason. I just can't figure out if it's because you need our help or because you're working with one of our enemies."

"Like a competitor or something? No one sent me here." Karolena could promise him that. She'd seen what Vladimir did to anyone suspected of snooping on him or his organization. Maybe the services the Shields provided were a little more serious than she'd realized or the clients a bit more complex than their small-town location would have led her to believe. "Unless it was fate or luck or karma, if you believe in any of those. I stand to gain a lot from my position here and I wouldn't jeopardize it by breaking the non-disclosure agreement James had me sign or by...whatever it is we might be about to do."

"Right." Legend nodded, then grabbed a fistful of his heathered gray T-shirt from between his shoulder blades. Before she could so much as process the motion, he'd whipped his shirt off and exposed a massive swath of tanned skin and the black hair coating it from his chest to the thick trail that disappeared beneath the waistband of his jeans.

It wasn't easy to think straight, never mind to talk. But she asked, "Just like that? You believe me?"

"In our line of work, there are a lot of times when you have to trust your gut. Please don't make me regret listening to mine now." Legend rubbed his ridged stomach as if it ached at the thought alone.

When had a man ever begged her for anything rather than threatening her if she so much as thought of betrayal? Karolena nodded. She had lied to these men plenty, but those falsehoods weren't intended to harm them, nor could they. Unless Vladimir tracked her down...

She'd come clean to the Shields eventually. If they proved it was wise. But until then, she reached for Legend with one hand and Tavish with the other.

Tavish fused his fingers with hers, his thumb rubbing slow circles over the back of her hand.

"You sure?" Legend hesitated a fraction of an instant before he did the same. "To be clear, you don't have to do this in order to stay safe or to keep your job. Fucking us is a bonus, not a condition of your employment."

"Swear you won't try to get me fired for screwing around on the clock?" Technically Karolena had finished her shift an hour ago, but she figured she owed time to account for the chaos she'd caused and then had to clean up.

Tavish grinned. "Pretty sure it's standard procedure around these parts. Besides, if Jordan or James cared, we'd be getting ourselves in trouble too by ratting you out. I can promise you we love what we do far too much to risk it."

Karolena swallowed hard, then nodded. So long as she wouldn't gamble her role and the protection it afforded... she was going to do this one greedy thing. All for herself. "If I didn't already want to sleep with you, promising I didn't have to would have convinced me I should. Let's just say it's been a long time since I've done something like this. Simply because I want to. So make it worth it, okay?"

Tavish descended on her before she finished her request. Legend brushed the hair from her face to keep it out of her mouth. When Tavish moved in to kiss her, she turned her head, directing his lips to her jaw and the extra-sensitive crook of her neck instead.

Legend seemed a bit disappointed, but he didn't encourage her to give more than she was comfortable with. Kissing was a familiarity she'd never shared with anyone. Not even Vladimir. He'd always skipped to the "good" parts. And now she found the thought of being face to face with someone impossibly personal.

Before she could get too into her head—and her memories—to enjoy what was about to go down, Karolena leaned so her forehead rested on Legend's collarbone. She towered over most women and a good deal of men, but Tavish had a few inches on her and Legend beat them both by even more.

In another universe, she might have become a ballerina like the ones she'd adored going to see with her mother when she was a little girl, even if they'd sat in the highest seats in the theater. Whether it was due to genetics, stress, or because what she ate was one of the very few things she could control—or all of the above— she'd struggled to gain weight. She'd certainly never developed the womanly curves she'd wished for when she'd first realized Vladimir's type wasn't a stick figure.

Do not think of that monster now.

Legend's warmth seeped into her and the steady thud of his heart grounded her.

"You can change your mind at any time." He arranged her hair so that it draped over his pecs, the ultra-light blond appearing nearly white against his bronzed skin.

"But I'm going to do my best to make sure you don't want to." Tavish kissed her shoulder before glancing up to see if she freaked out. When she didn't, he continued along it toward the column of her neck. Karolena whimpered as his mouth applied some pressure, sucking in just the right places to make shivers run up her spine.

Legend splayed his huge hand on her lower back, pinning her to him. The motion made it obvious precisely how much he hoped she went through with their liaison. Damn if he wasn't big all over. Karolena wondered if he would actually be able to make her feel...*something*, which was more than she could say of her ex in years.

Her heart raced when Tavish stepped closer, catching her between the two men.

Not because she was afraid, but because they chased her doubts from her mind and replaced them with anticipation. Not to be outdone by his partner, Tavish reached for the hem of Karolena's shirt. James had supplied her with several extra-soft V-necks that had the Shields logo printed over one side in the way of a uniform. She'd added a brand-new pair of black pants that were a cross between a yoga style and super-stretchy denim. They were comfortable and allowed her to move and bend as she was working.

Something about the thought of standing before them, bare, drew her up short. Silly when she was set on wringing every bit of pleasure from them that she could, but she at least wanted them to go first. Karolena tensed, wondering if they'd think she was too much effort if she let her quirks show.

Legend put his hand over Tavish's and prevented him from moving. "Wait a second. She seized up."

Tavish dropped his fingers and looked to her for guidance. Her hesitation evaporated. This was not how things had gone in the past. No one was forcing her to move faster than she wanted, mocking her for the fear that came with inexperience, or insisting it would all be fine if she'd just go along with it and stop being a baby.

"Thanks," she whispered to Legend before nuzzling his chest. His sturdy arms wrapped around her, hugging her and rocking slightly as Tavish did the same from behind. They held her close, bundled safely between them, and waited until her breathing settled before stroking her hair.

"We won't do anything you're uncomfortable with. Just tell us if we cross a line and we'll stop. Immediately." Tavish read her mind.

"What do you want to happen next?" Legend asked her.

As hypocritical as it was, she was dying to look at them. To feast on the results of their time in the mammoth gym she'd toured downstairs the day before. "Will you undress for me? Even if I want to keep my clothes on as much as possible for as long as possible?"

What if someone came to get them again? She didn't want to be scrambling to find her underwear and, frankly, her self-confidence was practically non-existent despite the way the two of them were touching her with reverent glides of their fingers over her skin.

It was a lot. Overwhelming if she exposed too much of herself to them too soon.

"Are you kidding? We basically have to beg Tavish to wear clothes. If it was up to him, he'd be strutting around this place naked all the time," Legend joked, helping to ease the tension even further.

"I can't wait for Bare Natural's grand opening." Tavish bent to unlace his boots, kicking them off so they clomped into the corner before he attacked his three-quarter-sleeved shirt, the arms of which were a light gray while the body was white. Three buttons at the neck allowed her a glimpse of the dusting of hair there. It matched the amber on his legs. Next he revealed the rest of his torso to her. He was trim where Legend was bulk. Both were masterpieces. "One of James's old Powertools crew has a naturist resort out by the Hot Rides garage on the edge of town. It's going to be great."

"Does that mean...?" Karolena looked to Legend for translation, never having heard that word in English before.

"That his tight Scottish ass will be tramping through the woods buck naked?" Legend laughed. "Yup."

Karolena couldn't imagine being that bold. Then again, she'd never suspected she'd be a very willing participant in a threesome on her first day of her new life.

In the time it took for them to tease him, Tavish had already worked the thick black leather belt from his kilt and dropped it on the floor, inspiring her shivers.

"Still okay?" Legend asked as his hand rode low on her back, resting on the top swell of her ass. His protective possessiveness did more to turn her on than the sight of them both half-naked.

She nodded before hugging him tight, tilting her face so she could soak in as much of Tavish as possible. Neither of the men moved to expose their lower halves. It surprised her when Legend looked to Tavish for direction. She would have assumed he would take charge of the pair but at most they were equals and she was starting to pick up on hints that it might be the other guy who held the reins when it came to fooling around.

Interesting.

Vladimir would never have taken direction from

anyone about her or how he used her. They couldn't possibly have been more different.

Tavish smiled at her then, extending his hand. "Let me take you somewhere comfortable. I know of a perfectly made bed right down the hall."

Did he really want to do this in one of their bedrooms?

No, that wouldn't do. The last thing she wanted was to make love in his personal space and forget that this was only a way to rebel and to experience the pleasure she'd seen men willing to kill, steal, and lie for. Instead of coming clean about how vulnerable she really was to them and their kindnesses, Karolena shook her head. "Too far. Here. Right here."

Legend looked to Tavish, then to the solid slab of a mammoth dining room table that stretched out in the open space beyond the pass-through kitchen. Black iron legs held up a polished chunk of tree with bark on the irregular edges.

When Tavish nodded, Legend wrapped his hands around her waist and plucked her from the floor. Though it was completely unnecessary to keep her steady in his grasp, she curled her legs around his hips and clung to him as he carried her to the other room.

Tavish strode in front of them, moving a chair out of the way at the head of the table so Legend could set her on it, her profile to the expanse of windows. The cross-section of the massive tree had been oiled and encased in some kind of shiny stuff that made it smooth, and a bitch to clean. She groaned.

"You okay?" Tavish asked, trailing the pad of his thumb down her cheek.

"Just thinking about how long it took me to get the fingerprints off this thing."

Legend laughed. "I'll pay you *not* to get rid of your ass-print so that I'm constantly reminded of the best thing I've ever eaten at this table."

"You think I'm going to let you devour her pretty pussy, do you?" Tavish hummed while he studied Karolena, as if he might be the one to taste her first.

And there it was. Proof that Tavish called the shots in their relationship. Or maybe that Legend enjoyed taking orders. She could see how the bigger, more thoughtful man might need someone to goad him into getting out of his head and throwing caution aside to take what he really wanted. Hell, she would never have had the guts to ask for this if Tavish hadn't been so overt in his desires.

By the same token, she figured Legend had a stabilizing effect on Tavish, keeping him from being too rough or directing some of his impetuous tendencies toward Legend instead of her. At least for now.

It was a nice mix and immediately she understood the draw of their tag-team approach.

A bird flew past to her left, making her head swivel in that direction. Exposed by the windows anyone could look through, and on display, she bit her lip but figured anyone peeking would get what they deserved. Still better to keep as much of her clothing on as possible, she reasoned.

"They're mirrored on the outside. No one can see us," Tavish promised her. "So sad for them."

Karolena didn't doubt they were about to put on one hell of a show.

She waited, expecting Tavish would tell her what he wanted next. Her mouth on his dick, she was sure. At least that's how it had always gone before. When he didn't rush her, instead standing beside Legend, as if to see what she would do with them, she decided to take matters into her own hands.

She reached for Legend's fly because he was closer. He let her unbutton it before slowly pulling down the zipper of his dark jeans and letting the pressure off his cock carefully, as if unwrapping a precious gift. She peeled the corners out and down, Legend assisting, before he shoved his pants over the bulk of his thighs so that they fell to the floor. With a kick, he launched them off to the side, where neither he nor Tavish would trip over them while otherwise occupied. He stood before her in boxer briefs that did nothing to hide the impression of his hard-on in the front of the black cotton. They looked nearly painted on, stretched to their limits in a band beneath his hips and the V of muscles pointing toward the prominent bulge.

"Impressive, isn't he?" Tavish asked as he edged closer, sliding his hand beneath the back of her shirt and rubbing from the base of her spine to her shoulders.

"Yeah." She'd certainly never seen a man like him before. "What if I can't handle him?"

"I can, and I'm happy to help." Tavish grinned. "Just enjoy. That's all you have to do."

Another point in favor of having them both there.

Tavish didn't try removing her shirt again, or even undo her bra, though his fingers traced her skin on either side of the utilitarian band. The men let her soak in the sight of Legend nearly naked before blasting her with the spotlight of their attention.

In minutes, they'd figured out more about her and her desires and hang-ups than her husband had after a decade. Or maybe Tavish simply gave a fuck about trying.

Either way, he put her at ease enough that she didn't

balk when his fingers paused on the clasp of her bra. She nodded to him and he opened it with a single, practiced flick. He slid his hand around to her front, petting her stomach before inching upward, causing her to arch into his touch.

"Should he get rid of those?" Tavish pointed with his chin at the scrap of fabric that was all the clothing Legend had left.

"Uh huh." She couldn't be more intelligible than that as she fought her drooping eyelids in response to the things Tavish was doing to her with his simultaneously soothing and enflaming caresses.

Legend paused a moment.

"You're not going to scare her," Tavish told his partner before turning to her. "Remember, you're only going to do what you're comfortable with, okay? No one's going to get upset or leave here unsatisfied."

Karolena nodded, then glanced up at Legend from beneath her lashes. "Show me."

Being fully dressed as he laid himself bare, completely exposed in front of her and Tavish, did something to Karolena. It made her feel like she was in charge for once. A potent switch from everything she'd done before.

And damn if Legend wasn't even more gorgeous than she'd realized. His muscles flexed as he stripped off his underwear and stepped out of them, flashing the side of his curvaceous, muscular ass when he turned and tossed them on top of his pants. He stood, his feet spread, balls hanging low between thighs at least as impressive as the tree trunk that had been sacrificed to construct their table. His cock, thick and heavy, stretched between his legs with no hope of standing on its own.

"Should he touch it? Or do you want to?" Tavish

murmured in her ear as his fingers slipped beneath the loosened cups of her bra to toy with the lower curve of her petite breasts.

"Let me," she replied to Tavish, but while looking into Legend's eyes.

5

———————

Legend stepped closer. Tavish took hold of one of Karolena's knees, coaxing it toward him, spreading her legs so that Legend could step between them while Tavish rubbed himself against the outside of her thigh. Her free hand reached for him, petting the bulge of his cock through his kilt. The pleated fabric folded nicely around him so she could squeeze him, measuring him with her fingers even as she fished for Legend.

Tavish thrust into her hold with an involuntary clench of his ass. He was as comfortable with the primal side of his nature as he had been making small talk at the party the night before. Civilized ferociousness, that's how she was coming to think of him, and Legend, and maybe all of the Shields.

Karolena's fingers landed on Legend's cock, which drew her full attention. He was so damn warm. An odd mixture of steely and soft that she found difficult to resist. Her fingers curled instinctively, grasping as much of him as she could hold.

He groaned, his cock jerking against her palm at their first contact. A pearl of precome emerged, encouraging her to squeeze him. He could take it. And seemed to like it plenty too.

It was surreal, not only seeing a man who wasn't Vladimir nude for the first time in her life, but to realize how different they were and how badly she wanted more than to play with him like this. If she was going to live out her fantasies for an afternoon, she intended to make the most of her temporary insanity.

While Karolena explored, rubbing and massaging Legend's shaft, then toying with the fluid at his tip, Tavish did some wandering of his own. His arm went higher up her shirt, exposing a strip of pale skin on her belly. Not too much, though. Certainly not enough that she was about to request he stop playing with her breasts.

When his hand finally cupped one fully, an easy handful for him, she sighed and pressed against him even as Legend was doing the same to her.

"I bet these tits are so perky. I'd love to see them someday. To suck on them while I'm fucking you." Tavish clearly enjoyed the idea. His cock was a solid rod beneath the fabric of his kilt.

She was too engrossed in the sensations already bombarding her to remind both him and herself that this was a one-time show. She couldn't afford to get too close to anyone.

"You like this?" Tavish asked, though she thought it was kind of obvious by the way she was squirming under the watchful stares of the two hottest men she'd ever met, tugging Legend closer by his dick even as she arched into Tavish's clutches.

"Yes." She turned her head, wishing she could taste his

parted lips, but there were some lines she refused to cross no matter how potent the longing.

"Want more?" Tavish asked, and Legend moaned. He certainly did. Was she ready to take him?

"Yes." She at least had to find out. It couldn't hurt any more than the times Vladimir had accosted her while she was asleep, completely unprepared, or unwilling but too resigned to fight him.

"Legend, get on your knees. Knock the edge off for her so she's relaxed and soaking wet." Tavish's accent thickened as his cock did the same in her grasp.

Did he mean...? Was he telling his partner to put his mouth on her like Vladimir had always made her do to him? Was that a thing?

Legend dropped to his knees, buried his face at her core and breathed deep through the fabric covering her most private parts. He hummed. "She's going to be delicious."

"You're so lucky to get to taste her." Tavish speared the fingers of his free hand into Legend's hair, which was a bit longer on the top than the sides. He took hold and pressed Legend's face against her crotch forcefully enough that it had to sting his scalp. But Legend didn't seem to mind and wrapped his fingers in the waistband of her pants.

That Legend trusted Tavish completely to know his limits made her more confident that they would respect hers as well.

"Can he take them off you?" Tavish asked, monitoring her reaction to his partner's intentions.

"What if someone comes? I'm supposed to working in here."

"Oh, someone is definitely going to come. Preferably a bunch of times."

Karolena snorted, but Tavish wasn't laughing. Legend hummed, sending vibrations through her that curled her toes in her utilitarian black slip-on shoes.

"We can get you off through your clothes if that's all you're comfortable with. We're not going to leave you hanging no matter what you decide," Tavish promised.

"Um, here, I can give him access." It sounded stiff and formal even to her given what they were about to share. But it was a limit she couldn't get past. For some dumb reason, that thin barrier made her feel less defenseless. They didn't pressure her for more.

Karolena toed off her shoes, then yanked the stretchy material down on one side, gyrating until she extracted her left leg. The pants remained half on, sheathing her other leg, clinging to it as if that made what she was doing any less obscene or irresponsible.

Legend and Tavish didn't seem to care about her false modesty. Not when Legend was inches from her pussy and the cheap pair of thin panties covering it. When she went to repeat her motion, Tavish stopped her. "You aren't real attached to those, are you? You're going to break something trying to contort out of them."

She shook her head no.

Legend grabbed the front and back panel, ripping the side seam and crotch wide open, leaving the scraps buried in her pants and under her butt.

"Oh."

Tavish laughed. "Trust me, you don't want to delay a moment more than necessary. His mouth is heaven."

That sounded like he knew from experience. The thought of watching a man suck another man's cock sent a tremor of pleasure through her. Especially if it was these two getting it on. If those sorts of relationships existed among Vladimir's men, they'd certainly been wise enough never to show a hint of it in front of him, and therefore her.

"I would like to find out for myself," Karolena said, her voice breathier than she'd ever heard it before. She cleared her throat, making Legend smile against her thigh.

Tavish, however, was a little more clear-headed. "Do you mean what Legend specifically is capable of or is this new for you?"

"Uh." Should she lie? What was one more whopper on the pile? Would they stop if they knew how little experience she really had compared to them? Would they be disappointed when they realized all she really knew how to do during sex was lie there and take it?

Apparently her hesitation was answer enough for them.

"Holy shit," Legend muttered before looking up at Tavish. "Please don't make me wait to show her everything she's been missing."

Tavish looked a bit angry. At her? "Don't you dare. Eat her until she comes all over your face."

Karolena's body gathered at the thought alone. Except it also made her nervous. "I don't know if I can—"

"I do." Tavish aimed some of his authority at her then, but not in a way that frightened her. He reassured and made promises she hoped he could keep. "Relax. Let us take care of you. There's no hurry and no expectations, okay? Stop thinking and feel what we can do."

Legend petted her inner thighs and rumbled, "Enjoy and the rest will happen, or not. No pressure."

"But I'd bet my entire cut of our bonus from last night that you won't be able to hold out long beneath his tongue. I never can." Tavish smirked, confirming her suspicions.

Karolena sighed and did as they instructed.

"That's right," Tavish purred before guiding Legend's head to her bare flesh.

Then he didn't need any more encouragement. He licked her lightly, getting her used to the feel of his tongue on her skin. It was warm and wet and so soft she instinctively spread her legs wider to give him better access.

"Hell yes." Tavish cheered them on. He let go of Legend long enough to rearrange her legs so they draped over his partner's shoulders. Then he attended to himself. He reached beneath his kilt and grabbed hold of his erection, lifting the fabric so it was obvious he hadn't been wearing anything beneath. He reclaimed her hand and drew it to him, encouraging her to pick up where she'd left off on Legend, instead stroking him.

Legend cut his eyes to Tavish, who said, "You can jerk yourself, but slow. Don't get too excited. We're going to save that cock of yours for Karolena."

At least if they kept their word, she'd already have found satisfaction by the time they advanced to intercourse. Maybe that would make it less unpleasant when Legend finally sought pleasure within her for himself. Fair enough after how much attention they were already willing to shower on her.

Tavish let his kilt rest on top of his cock, which jutted up from beneath it. She thought it seemed even more obscene with him semi-dressed than if he was as bare as Legend. But his in-between state didn't last long. As she took over for him, working his cock, which was longer than Vladimir's but not as thick as Legend's, Tavish attacked the straps at his sides until he was able to unwind the kilt from his narrow waist.

And then the guys were both there, bare before her, unafraid of putting themselves on display for her greedy stares and touches.

Karolena mimicked Tavish's earlier hold on Legend's hair, using it to encourage him to linger on spots that fanned the fire growing low in her belly. When Tavish leaned in, she began to pump his cock in time to the swirls of Legend's tongue, which were traveling upward toward the top of her slit.

Tavish put his hand over hers, showing her how he liked to be handled—a few rapid strokes before a couple slow ones. Then he dragged her fingers lower until they trailed over his balls.

When he groaned, she did too. Both because of the rapture Legend gifted her with and also because it thrilled her to know she could have a similar impact on them. Vladimir had often told her how much better it was when he slept with other women and how cold and unadventurous she was. To realize that this pair of men had no complaints...it was the most potent turn-on of all.

Tavish used her hand to jerk himself off. They watched Legend devouring her, sucking on her clit in between passes of his tongue while he rubbed his own cock. As Karolena began to feel herself open and grow aroused, something she hadn't ever experienced so intensely, Legend burrowed deeper, pressing his tongue to her opening and a bit inside before returning to spoil her clit with kisses, licks, and soft sucks.

Karolena stared at him in wonder, watching him operate between her thighs like the master he was. All the while Tavish thrust into her fingers, now curled tightly around him. He fucked her hand, giving her some idea of what it might be like once he fitted himself inside her.

She wished they would hurry, that they would claim her.

But they refused to be hasty. They acted as if they were going to spend as much time screwing her that afternoon as her ex had in the entire decade of their forced marriage.

"Is he doing a good job, Karolena?" Tavish asked, the warmth of his breath on her neck as he braced his forehead on her cheek.

"Mmmm," she moaned, and assumed it was answer enough. Her eyes closed as she absorbed the sparkles they had sent through her veins, so she didn't anticipate the contact with his palm until he returned it to her abdomen, stroking gently.

"You're so beautiful," Tavish told her. "Your cheeks are flushed and your nipples are hard. Do you want me to pinch them for you? Rub them so you feed Legend your first orgasm for today?"

Karolena wanted to question his bold assessment, but she didn't bother. Instead she opened her eyes and hoped he could see the plea in them.

"That's what I thought." Tavish smiled, though it was sharper now that it was seeped in arousal at least as potent as her own.

She stroked his shaft a bit frantically, noticing her hand getting slick from the fluid leaking from him, but he backed away until she slowed down again.

"Not so fast," Tavish said before returning his palm to her breast and pinching lightly. "I have a lot of self-control, but even I can't resist the two of you for too long.

And I want to do a hell of a lot more than shoot my load on your fingers."

Karolena couldn't say if it was the thought of being able to push him over the edge or the mental image of his hot seed pouring over her hand or maybe the pressure from his fingers on her breast, which was both sharp and sweet at the same time. But all of those things, coupled with Legend's incessant lapping in all the right places, caused something to blossom within her.

Her spine arched and she unraveled in their arms.

They kept their promises when they made her come, the epic release hard and long enough that she saw stars. Wonder flowed through her as she soaked in as much of the awe as possible while trying to keep breathing, even if it was in ragged gasps. And still, they kept touching her, letting her down gently, though not all the way.

When she mewled their names, barely able to catch her breath, Tavish was there. "I told you he's good at that, didn't I?" He chuckled a bit before kissing her forehead lightly.

For an instant, she considered tipping her face up. No. Even when she'd thrown so much caution to the wind, she wasn't ready to be that daring. So instead she nodded. "Yeah."

Legend smiled against her sopping core. "That's only the beginning, Karolena. I'm going to put my fingers in you now. Stretch you so Tavish can show you how much better it can get."

She looked to Tavish, who agreed. "He knows me well. Would you like another?"

Surprisingly, she did. The first burst of ecstasy had been overwhelming and so unusual it had caught her off guard. This time she would savor it. "Yes. Please."

6

———

Legend groaned against Karolena. He bit the inside of her thigh lightly, just enough to get her attention before shifting so that his hand glided along the skin there, soothing the impression of his teeth before continuing inward. When he fit the blunt tip of one finger to her opening, she tried to shift her body so she could engulf him in a single motion.

Tavish pressed down on her sternum, keeping her in place on their table. "Not like that. Let him ease into you. We're not going to hurt you or let you do it to yourself. Easy, Karolena. There's plenty more. I swear."

She believed him.

So she relaxed, and when she did, Legend's hand shifted inward, pressing the barest bit inside her. Her muscles clenched around his middle finger, hugging it as he spiraled deeper, retreating a bit when he met resistance, then returning over and over, carefully fitting them together.

Tavish surprised her by mimicking Legend's movements, but against her mouth. He stuck his arm through the V-neck of her shirt and pressed his middle finger to her parted lips. She opened wider, letting him insert it in her mouth then sucking on it when he did.

Having something to hold and lick and suck gave her an outlet for her restless energy while Legend probed her with first one and then a second finger. He scissored them within her, spreading her, pressing against the ring of muscles at her entrance and coaxing it to open for him when all it wanted was to clench and strangle him every time he ramped her higher.

So when he added the suction of his mouth on her clit to the slow pump of his digits within her, she thought she might explode on the spot. She bit Tavish's finger, making him chuckle. "I know. He's amazing. You can let go whenever you're ready. We'll be here to catch you and keep making it better."

It would have been impossible for it to feel any more wonderful than it already did. Karolena's toes curled and she shifted so her socked feet planted on Legend's massive shoulders, giving her some leverage to lift her hips and fuse her pussy more tightly to his mouth.

By the time he unfurled a third finger and began to wedge it into her alongside the other two, Karolena was trying not to pant. Tavish withdrew his hand from her mouth and dragged the wet tip of his finger down her throat to her breasts.

When he kneaded them, squeezing and pinching, she didn't stand a chance at resisting.

"Damn, she's so tight." Legend lifted up just long enough to warn Tavish. "She's going to come again. Any second."

"Perfect," he murmured, though if it was to her or Legend or both, she didn't know or care. Karolena threw her head back as Legend plunged as deeply inside her as he could reach. He curled his fingers within her, pressing on places she hadn't even known existed in her own body, triggering her second orgasm.

She might have lost control and crashed to her back on the table, but Tavish was there, hugging her to his heaving chest as she surrendered to the moment and the absolute delight they were infusing into every cell of her body. He held her as she spasmed, crushing Legend's hand with the undulations of her pussy.

And when, sometime later, he lowered her gently to the table, she forced herself to blink her eyes open. Just in time to see Tavish cover Legend's hand with his own and ease it from inside her. Karolena missed having him lodged within her, but she hoped that Tavish intended to replace the treat he'd stolen from her.

His cock was ruddy. The veins stood out in relief on his shaft. But still he didn't crack. Instead, he took Legend's hand and brought it to his mouth, sucking on his fingers like she had Tavish's so recently. He cleaned every bit of her glistening arousal from Legend's digits, then cupped the back of Legend's neck.

Tavish drew Legend to him then shared the mingled taste of him and her with Legend in a searing kiss. Their cocks stabbed at each other as the duo pressed together from lips to knees. Their passion and willingness to be so open to whatever form it took inspired her.

Karolena's hand wandered to between her legs and she recreated some of Legend's wizardry on herself as she studied them exchanging the flavor of her arousal between them. Karolena cried out as an aftershock or maybe a third small orgasm crashed over her.

Tavish whipped toward her. Both he and Legend

grinned as they realized their display had impacted her. They had no idea how much. This day was going to change her life. Forever.

She was never again going to settle when she knew this was possible.

And technically, they hadn't even fucked her yet.

Tavish disappeared, but only for a moment or two. At least, it seemed that way to her. Because she lunged for Legend, wanting to return the favor. She nudged him to the very edge of the table, swinging around so her mouth was level with his cock. But before she could wrap her lips around it, he put his hand on her shoulder. "No, thanks."

Huh? Karolena glanced up at him, confusion and shame dampening her lingering excitement. Familiar rejection threatened to snuff out the high they'd lifted her to. "Why? Do you only like it when Tavish does it?"

Legend chuckled and cupped her cheek. "Nah. I would enjoy it too much. And Tavish won't be happy with me if I come before I'm buried deep inside you. It would only take a moment right now, Karolena. Let him take care of you until I can get myself together again."

Karolena blinked. "You enjoyed...what you did to me...*that* much?"

"You're so soft, and sweet, hot and tight, and...*damn*. Yeah, Karolena. I loved every second." Legend spun her around then, and flipped her, so that her half-clothed ass was in the air. Her cheek rested on the cool surface of the table, her face tipped so she could watch what he was doing out of the corner of her eye. He dipped his fingers into her pussy, then withdrew them for another taste of what he'd done to her. Her thighs quaked, but he held her hip so that she didn't tip over as he kept her wired for Tavish.

When Tavish returned, condoms in his fist, his eyes bright and fixated on where she and Legend met, another aftershock rolled through her.

Tavish flashed a wolfish smile, then carefully opened one of the foil packets. While she expected him to put it on himself, he didn't. He reached over and rolled it down Legend's thick cock with enough familiarity that she was certain it wasn't the first time he'd done it.

Karolena moaned.

"You like seeing my hands on him?" Tavish asked, though he obviously knew the answer.

She nodded, incapable of speech when they had wound her so tight.

"Maybe some other time I'll let you watch me fuck him."

Legend groaned and gritted his teeth. "You're not helping, Tavish."

The other man finished fitting the condom before he pinched Legend's nipple. "I've got you. Both of you. No one's leaving here hungry. Let me warm her up for you and then you can get in there and show her why we call you Legend."

Tavish shooed Legend's fingers from his cock when he would have returned the favor and wrapped himself in a condom as well. "I'm going to fuck you first. We'll work up to the big guy, huh? Besides, it's better when we take turns. We can last as long as you like then. So take as much as you want. There will be enough."

Karolena swallowed hard, though not in fear. She was sure they wouldn't cause her more than discomfort, and if she called it, they would stop outright. Now it was pure desire driving her onward.

Tavish clamped her hips in his hands. "Feet on the floor. I'm not that tall."

He was plenty. In every regard.

Karolena couldn't quite coordinate her limbs, so Legend helped to arrange her for his partner. He lowered her legs so she was standing then pressed lightly between her shoulder blades until she folded over the edge of the table. She crossed her arms, her wrists stacked, then laid the side of her face on them. The glassy surface beneath her cooled her breasts and the rest of her front through her shirt for a moment.

At least until something rounded and hard and hot notched in the opening of her pussy. She arched so her ass was thrust back at Tavish, and he didn't disappoint. He grabbed her cheeks and spread her open, providing himself plenty of room to work and to observe as her pussy began to swallow his cock.

She cried out, though not in pain or anything resembling it. Intense bliss shot from her core outward as Tavish leaned over her and raked his teeth across her shoulder.

"Fuck. You feel so good on my dick."

Legend was there, by their sides, witnessing Tavish's penetration as his shaft bored into her. He scanned her expression as she welcomed his friend inch by inch. His vigilance reassured her that if he saw the slightest wince or a hint of panic in her eyes that he would have shut Tavish down in an instant.

But none of that was necessary because once she got a sample of his cock within her, she needed the whole thing.

"How is she?" Tavish asked, his brogue fraying as he strove for control.

"Incredible." Legend beamed as he dragged his fingers down the length of her spine. "Ready for more. Go ahead. Fuck her, Tavish."

Karolena couldn't believe it, but it was true. Tavish was fatter even than Legend's three fingers and certainly larger than her ex. However, she didn't suffer even a twinge of pain as Tavish sank balls-deep into her. The revelation thrilled her even as it planted a seed of sadness in her heart for her to examine later. If two strangers cared more than her asshole ex had about her comfort and pleasure, that meant her "love life" had been even more twisted than she'd realized.

Legend stood guard beside Tavish, unbothered that he and Tavish made contact as Tavish began to shuttle in and out of her. Legend kept rubbing her back, checking in with her to make sure she was comfortable.

Tavish began slow, filling her with long, deep strokes that had her splaying her hands on the table. But when he picked up the pace, his torso slapping against her ass filling the open room with lewd, wet sounds, Legend must have realized she was going to need a bit of assistance to keep up with his partner. He reached around behind Tavish, pausing on the way to cup the other man's balls.

Tavish snarled something that was likely a Scottish curse, his stride hitching. "Don't play with fire. Rub her instead."

"I was getting there." Legend winked at her.

"Now is not the time to be smart with me. Or I'll make you suffer before I let you have a turn," Tavish threatened, though without much heat.

Legend didn't antagonize Tavish. He left his partner to focus on fucking Karolena while he went for her clit. He tapped it first, then started rubbing circles around it in time to Tavish's thrusts.

The introduction of the additional stimulation weakened her knees. She might have slid to the floor in a giddy puddle if Legend hadn't been there to support her. He braced her, propping her up against his hip and holding her still for Tavish to plow.

It took everything Karolena had to hold on. Physically and mentally.

The release they were giving her was beyond what she had realized she'd needed. The massive highs and lows of her escape—terror, hope, desperation—amplified her response, providing her a way to vent the emotions she'd previously kept so tightly locked inside.

Karolena cried out, her nails clawing at the table while her face smooshed against it. Legend tried to help by using the hand not busy rubbing her clit to brace her neck. But the careful grip on her throat, though not violent in the least, triggered a flashback that made her thrash beneath him and Tavish. This time not in ecstasy.

Legend noticed immediately. "Hey, Karolena. You're fine. I was trying to help, but I'm letting go. Be careful of your face near the table, okay? No one's going to harm you here."

Tavish halted his rocking motion. He remained deeply embedded in her, pulsing forward and backward the barest bit, as if he was using every bit of his restraint to put the brakes on his body when they'd both been so engrossed in what they did to each other.

The dearth of sensation shocked her back to reality and the present. They weren't going to turn on her, even when she was most at their mercy.

Karolena looked into Legend's worried face and attempted a smile. "I know. Sorry."

"There's nothing to apologize for." Tavish petted her flanks. "Are you okay?"

"I will be if you let this go and pick up where you left off." Karolena buried her face in her hands. "I was getting close."

"I could tell." Tavish groaned as he began again, this time with more finesse and less urgency. "Probably for the best we took a break or I might have flown with you."

"Doubtful." Legend looked shocked when he realized Tavish wasn't joking. "Already?"

"Hey, tell me you can do better when you're in here." Tavish grimaced. "We can talk about the rest later. For now, action is going to have to be enough."

"It is." Karolena sighed as endorphins chased bad memories from her mind.

Legend resumed playing her, redoubling his efforts as Tavish nailed that sweet spot inside her over and over. It took only a few more strokes and she was there, grabbing for that whiteout of rapture that would take away everything but that moment and absolute pleasure.

"Go ahead, Karolena," Tavish cooed to her. "Let go of everything but this."

She did and she flew.

Her body spasmed around him. She hugged him a few times before he ripped himself away with another unintelligible phrase. Legend supplied his fingers for her to hold as her body rippled around them. Had Tavish been about to join her? And if so, why had he stopped?

They couldn't really mean for her to do this over and over. Was that even possible? Would she survive it if so?

Her heart raced and her body throbbed. And still, she didn't want it to end.

Certainly not when Legend hadn't taken anything for himself. As soon as she could draw a lungful of air, she planned to tell him so. But the guys beat her to it.

Tavish took over holding her, then told Legend, "Get on the table. She can't stand anymore."

Legend sprang up beside her, then stretched out on his back, surprisingly agile for someone so muscular. He drew her over him like a blanket, her thighs splaying on either side of one of his. She rubbed her pussy on the curve of his quad as she rode out the orgasm they'd given her.

"Damn, Karolena." He finger-combed her hair and admired her where she draped over him. He was like the world's best teddy bear.

"You have no idea how badly I needed this," she confessed quietly.

"I'm getting that sense." Legend cuddled her close, which was fine until he shifted as if he was going to roll them both over.

Despite their careful handling and how thoroughly they'd already reshaped her view of what a healthy sexual encounter could look like, she wasn't quite ready to be pinned down, trapped beneath the thrusting body of a man she had no chance of escaping.

So instead, she curled her hands on either side of his ribcage and shoved while twisting her body in the opposite direction. He resisted at first until he realized she wasn't playing.

When Karolena stiffened in Legend's hold, Tavish asked. "Have you had enough?"

"It's not that." Karolena willed herself not to fight what

was happening between them but only to shape it into a positive foundation for the rest of her life. "I just...would rather be on top."

Tavish grinned. "Legend will never bitch about that. He loves to be ridden."

Legend didn't deny it. Instead, he flopped to his back, his feet and arms splayed, his cock resting thick on his rock-hard belly. "Use me however you want."

She climbed upward so that she could straddle him, creating a lewd centerpiece for their table. Tavish reached out and encircled the base of Legend's cock, pointing it straight at the ceiling.

Would he really fit? They were about to find out.

"Go slow," Tavish warned her. "Let me help and if it's too much, it's fine. I can take over."

"Hell, I'm about to come if someone sneezes in my direction." Legend groaned, his feet restless on the table. "Get on top and rub that pussy over me. I'll be flooding this fucking condom in thirty seconds."

Tavish looked to Karolena, giving her the opportunity to take the out.

Absolutely not.

Karolena planted one palm on the table and leaned back, opening herself to Legend and to the ecstasy he was about to deliver, because if his mouth had been spectacular, she knew fucking him would be divine. There was no way a man made like him, who clearly knew how to use what he'd been given, was going to let her down.

Especially not if Tavish had anything to say about it.

He wrapped one arm around her back and guided her to Legend's dick. He supported her weight and kept her from sinking too quickly when her body found Legend's and began to sheath his cock. She smothered him, encasing him in her stretched pussy.

"Ah!" Her strangled cry was enough to communicate what she needed. More of them.

Tavish guided her down bit by bit, letting gravity fuse her with Legend.

He pounded his fist on the table. "Son of a bitch!"

With his middle finger, Tavish checked their fit, running the tip of it at the intersection of their bodies. "He's filling you up, isn't he?"

"Yes." Karolena planted her hands on Legend's chest and wriggled a bit on top of him, trying to rub him against the places he and Tavish had so easily located within her.

He groaned. Tavish adjusted his grip, cupping her hips. "Try this."

He coached her through a pattern that made both her and Legend cry out in unison. So she concentrated on repeating it herself over and over. As she did, she looked down.

Karolena watched Legend's cock pressing between her legs, within her, her pussy swallowing him whole as she rode him. It felt so different to be the one driving the action, certain that if she said she was done, even right now, that he would let her leave.

Power and pleasure blended, making her toss her head back, her platinum hair cascading from the bun into loose waves. Unfettered, free, just like her.

With one final burst of adrenaline, Karolena ground over Legend, launching them both toward an inevitable peak. Legend's eyes flew to Tavish's.

"Go ahead. I'll take care of her. You know I will," he reassured Legend, who was quivering beneath her. The irrefutable proof of how desperately he craved release within her ratcheted Karolena's desire to a whole new level.

"Not necessary." She bucked as her body gathered on the precipice of release.

"Even better." Tavish shoved them both over the edge when he demanded, "Then come, Karolena. He won't be able to stop himself from joining you. Take him there with you."

Could she really do that? Be enough to trigger his orgasm?

Apparently her body wanted nothing more than to find out. Karolena screamed as the climax hit her this time. Shuddering, she would have tipped, smashing onto Legend if it wasn't for Tavish catching her. He held her as his roommate shouted, "Fuck! Yes, fuck!"

Each of his words was punctuated by a sharp thrust upward and, she'd bet, a pulse of his seed jetting into the condom he wore. Legend roared as he emptied himself deep inside her, her body milking him dry.

Tavish settled her on Legend's chest, letting them float together as they absorbed the bliss they'd created together. He backed away to the chair they'd displaced and sank onto it. She didn't realize what he was doing at first until his soft grunts shook her from the daze her string of orgasms had induced.

"Legend." She shook him until his eyelids fluttered open a bit. "Help me. Please."

7

Karolena watched as Legend's eyes flew open then, and he scanned the room for the source of Karolena's concern.

"Oh hell no." Legend refused to let Tavish take matters into his own hands after he'd orchestrated so much pleasure for them.

But Karolena could hardly budge, never mind hover over him with enough coordination to make him come. Neither could she stomach the idea of letting him overwhelm her by being on top, even now.

Legend slipped his hand between them and held on to his condom as he disconnected their bodies. Both of them moaned at the loss.

"I'm fine. This is only going to take a few seconds." Tavish's mouth was a tight slash. His knees spread wide as he rubbed himself furiously.

Legend tipped Karolena to one side, then rolled to the other. It took him a moment to find his balance, then he plucked her from the table and carried her to Tavish. "You're sure?"

"Yeah." She held her arms out to Tavish as Legend put her in his lap. "I just...I'm tired."

Exhausted was more like it. Being on the run would have been enough, but add on top a hard day's work, then a marathon sex session. Yeah, she was running on fumes.

"I've got you." Legend stood behind her, his hands beneath her arms, holding her weight as Tavish guided her lower half to his lap.

"Fuck yes, Karolena. Let him use your body to fuck us both until we can't hold out a moment longer. I'm going to fall with you this time."

If she'd ever needed motivation, that was it. To know that she had equal sway over her lovers. To make them feel so much that they would unravel.

Legend held her steady as she squirmed into place, settling onto Tavish easily. Her pussy slid over his sheathed cock. She wondered what it would feel like if he was bare instead.

Maybe someday she would get to find out.

Karolena was so lost in the passion they generated in each other that she didn't realize she was already thinking of next time and the time after that when she'd only intended to have an afternoon of no-strings sex.

Tavish didn't try to pull her down to him. He didn't force her to make out with him or invade her space. He let Legend bring them both indescribable pleasure with her body being the tool to make it happen.

Karolena loved the sensations caused by Tavish's blunt head pressing, pressing, then sinking deep within her, spreading her for the shaft that followed. She hugged him tight as she worked over him, driving him into her deeper with each bit her thighs relaxed.

"I can hold you higher if it's not comfortable," Legend offered.

"No way. I want all of him." Karolena purred as she swallowed Tavish, taking more and more until her pussy kissed his balls.

"You're about to have every drop," he growled.

Karolena hadn't thought it possible, but it seemed her body responded to the men bracketing her in ways she'd never imagined. She raced to one final summit, chasing the fireworks that lit within her at every nudge of Tavish's cock against her hyper-stimulated nerves. Frantic, she couldn't hardly breathe, never mind harness the practiced grace of her dance classes. When she tried to enhance Legend's measured motions, she nearly dislodged Tavish with an uncoordinated jerk.

"Whoa, careful." Legend noticed and refused to let her injure herself or his partner. He clasped his hands around her waist tighter and moved her in a more measured rhythm that didn't sacrifice on the pacing.

"Fuck." Tavish's head thrashed, setting his hair in motion like flames around his face.

"You've got to put him out of his misery, Karolena." Legend chuckled even as he helped her grind on Tavish before lifting her up again. He was essentially using her like a toy to fuck his friend and something about that only ramped her up higher. "He's waiting for you to come before he finishes."

How was that even possible?

Their stamina had started to make Karolena wonder if they didn't need whatever this was between them as desperately as she did in that moment.

The knowledge that they did was enough to light her up from her fingertips to her toes. A pulse of energy went through her, gathering before exploding outward. She tossed her head back and screamed as her body expelled every bit of terror and shame they'd converted to rapture instead.

Tavish shouted her name and clutched her to his chest as he pumped upward in a string of harsh jabs that coincided with his own release. He wrapped himself around her, sheltering her, which was far more dangerous than any physical venting.

Because Karolena wanted nothing more than to stay in his arms.

Which was why, long before she would otherwise have budged, she peeled herself from his grasp on legs so wobbly Legend had to assist, then sank to the floor as her insides still pulsed.

Spent, Legend crashed beside her and Tavish melted, his head lolling backward on the chair as the milky, opaque condom settled around his deflating cock.

At least they looked nearly as wrecked as she felt.

What the hell had they just done to each other?

Karolena refused to believe it was anything other than an explosive bodily reaction inspired by years of starving herself of attention or affection or sexual stimulation. That's all she could afford for it to be.

So when Tavish came around a bit and frowned at her and Legend sprawled on the floor, she knew she had to retreat before things could become more serious than she would survive.

"Let me take you both to bed." Tavish peeled himself from the chair, disposed of both his and Legend's condoms, then returned with two dish towels dampened with warm water.

When he offered one to her, she took it from him

rather than letting him clean her as he seemed to intend. No way could she stand to be that intimate with him or anyone else.

Legend froze as he noticed the shift in the energy surrounding them.

"You're not staying, are you?" Tavish asked quietly.

"We've had our fun. And it was. Honestly. Now I should go back to my place. Alone." Karolena didn't try to be as careful with him as he'd been with her. But she saw it. The pain she caused when she retreated. She wouldn't make that mistake a second time, so she added, "This can't happen again."

Legend made a sound that reminded her of a wounded animal. She thought she heard him mutter, "Thought we'd gotten lucky like the rest. Stupid."

Karolena scooted farther away from them both to avoid rushing to their sides and soothing the sting of her disavowal.

"I'm afraid we can't let you leave." Tavish grimaced.

"What the hell do you mean?" Karolena found the strength to stand then, jamming her leg back in her pants. Good thing she'd left them mostly on after all.

"James told us to keep an eye on you. Why'd you lie, Karolena?" Tavish shocked her.

"You know?" How much had they figured out about her past and why she'd shown up in Middletown? "Was this all some attempt to soften me up? You bastards! Do you get paid extra for having to fuck me? Are you going to send me back?"

Karolena should have realized two men like them could never truly want a woman like her. She scrambled away from them, backing all the way through the kitchen while they approached, their hands out. She crashed into her cleaning cart hard enough to leave a bruise on her hip. Good, it would remind her how real the hazard was of believing anyone. Especially wicked men like them.

How stupid to forget. To be blinded by their sexy bodies and the things they could do with them.

"Calm down." Tavish snatched his kilt off the floor and wound it around his hips. He closed the gap between them and she knew even if it was unlocked, she'd never make it out the door before he caught her. Besides, where would she run to? There was nowhere to hide. "It might be my job to make sure nothing happens to you or anyone else around here, but what we just shared was honestly my pleasure."

"*Our* pleasure," Legend corrected.

Karolena realized they'd fucked her in more ways than the obvious. Because it turned out she wasn't the sort of woman who could separate sex from the emotional impacts of blinding pleasure on her mind as well as her body. Even if the people she'd slept with were liars and a threat to everything she'd thought she was embracing.

She didn't expect she'd be able to slip past them and escape again, but for her own sanity, she had to try. Except just as she turned toward the exit to bolt, Legend's phone chirped behind her. Tavish ignored it, sprinting in her direction and slamming his hand on the door to keep it closed even as she realized it was indeed electronically locked and she didn't know how to open it from the inside.

Shit!

Karolena rounded on him. She lifted her fists, though she'd never hit a person in her life. Before she even registered Tavish's intent, he'd grasped her wrists and pinned them to the door above her head. Not violently.

Without hurting her. But so deftly that there was no way she could break loose.

"Gonna help me out here?" Tavish asked over his shoulder at Legend, who was reading something on his phone.

The flush faded from his cheeks as he leveled a gaze at Tavish and her, caught in his grasp. Entirely differently from how he'd held her so recently. "Ruby works fast."

"They need us downstairs again?" Tavish's mouth pinched at the corners.

"Yeah, but not only you and me. All three of us."

Karolena's hands and feet went numb and her ability to speak vanished. "Me? What do the Shields want with me? I'm sorry I lied. I had to. Don't you understand?"

"Not at all. We'd really appreciate it if you'd tell us yourself what's going on rather than having to hear it from our colleagues." Legend seemed far calmer than Tavish. Or maybe it was their proximity that allowed her to take in every clench of his jaw and the betrayal in his very green eyes.

He didn't threaten her, but she sensed an ultimatum in his question. She could come clean, or she could lose his faith. It was probably for the best. They'd proven to her in just one romp, that they were far more of a threat to her than Vladimir had ever been.

Because after that taste, she might already be addicted to them. But if they truly didn't know the whole story, then they likely weren't working for her ex and maybe... just maybe...they could help.

"I'm only doing this once." She yanked against his hold.

To her surprise, Tavish released her. So she reached behind her to fasten her bra, then retrieved and slipped into her shoes. In under ten seconds, she was ready to destroy the tenuous link they'd begun to forge.

When she returned to the doorway, Legend and Tavish flanked her. This time they seemed more like prison guards than bodyguards.

After they heard what she had to say for herself, would they be friends or foes?

And how could she fight back if they were no longer on her side?

Damn it.

Her past was going to haunt her forever, no matter how far or how fast she ran.

8

———————

Tavish checked his phone in case Legend had sent him a message he didn't want to communicate out loud. Instead he saw a group text to both of them from Ruby.

I know who she is. Get down here. Now. Bring her with you.

Damn it. That meant Karolena was someone. Not just an insignificant woman lying on her resume for reasons like having gotten fired from her previous job after being late too often or some other petty shit.

Fuck!

He had so badly wanted Karolena to be uninvolved in their world of subterfuge and darkness. Inexperienced not only in cleaning or good sex but also in the horrors the Shields had witnessed from a level of humanity so low that regular people never even knew it existed, never mind attempted to exterminate it.

They'd seen the worst of the worst.

And Ruby's text meant Karolena was part of it.

He glanced at her in his peripheral vision as he and

Legend marched her into the elevator, but she never lifted her dazed stare from the floor. She knew she was busted as surely as he did. Again, not a good sign.

At least they'd gotten to fuck before the illusion was shattered. His dick wouldn't be able to get it up for her if she turned out to be a mole, someone who'd attempted to strike at his newfound family. He'd lived through that once and would send her to their basement before he'd let her harm a single person at Shields.

It didn't matter how deeply she'd rocked him when she'd shattered around him minutes earlier or how convincing she'd been when she'd sworn she hadn't been sent there by an enemy.

Tavish breathed through flared nostrils as he tried not to assume the worst. Forced himself not to compare her to the traitor who'd stolen his heart and his better judgment last time. When his relatives had paid for his lapse and he'd sworn never to be so stupid again.

Usually Legend kept him from indulging his impulsive nature. This time, they'd both felt the pull to Karolena. Could that have been intentional? Could the attraction have been calculated?

If so, she was the best actress he'd ever seen, A-list stars included.

As they sank toward the ground floor, Legend glowered at their reflections, not very subtly assessing Tavish's mental state. Tavish met his partner's gaze, hoping the other man got the *Piss off!* vibes he blasted in Legend's direction. He was fine. He would do his job no matter what Ruby had found out about their sham maid.

Karolena surprised Tavish by leading the way out of the elevator, her spine straighter than the mop handle she'd clutched so tightly earlier. She'd been legitimately afraid they'd ax her for her fuck-up. Why did she really want to be there so badly?

It certainly wasn't to clean their damn floors. Who had put her in their paths?

Legend extended his arm and held his hand, palm up, gesturing for her to enter the conference room where the rest of the team was already assembled.

The gathering was hushed, kind of a miracle since the team was usually shooting the shit, joking around, and talking smack before a briefing and the start of another high-stakes adventure. They weren't used to having a saboteur in their midst. Not here at home.

Everyone swiveled in their direction with the focus they reserved for missions.

Definitely not good.

"Son of a bitch," Legend muttered under his breath.

Jordan rose as they entered and pointed to three seats near the head of the table. "Karolena, come sit. I need to talk to you about your background check."

Tavish wouldn't be surprised if Jordan knew every detail about her down to the color of the underwear Legend had destroyed. But he was smart enough that he wouldn't give any of it away. He'd test her first, see if she was truthful about whatever she disclosed.

That was going to make the process take longer. They were going to have to suffer through a story from her that could be absolute bullshit and he wouldn't know until the end. He could make it a game to test his own lie-dar, since he'd lost faith in his ability to detect the dishonesty of a pretty woman. Better if he could have gotten a direct briefing, but he knew how the game was played.

So did Legend. His partner huffed out a sigh as he

sank into a chair on Karolena's right side even as Tavish did the same on her left.

"Am I about to be fired before I've finished my first day?" She shrugged as if it was inevitable. "Your loss. You should have seen the job I did on their apartment."

Tavish couldn't help a wry chuckle at that, considering the silhouette of her ass was stamped all over their dining table.

"Is there reason for us to let you go?" Jordan asked, though Tavish was well aware that if she'd tried to pull anything on them, the only place she'd be heading was to their basement. Termination meant something far worse to the Shields than a break in employment.

The thought made him sick. He clutched his gut. Not because he had a single shred of remorse for the people he'd ended. They were evil enough to justify it or he wouldn't have gotten involved. But because he had clicked with Karolena from the start and she'd fit him like she'd been custom-made for him...and Legend.

After watching agent after agent find their perfect counterparts, some stupid part of him had been hopeful that maybe he and Legend could cross paths with a woman who would bind them together for good.

Karolena's shoulders slumped then. If she was faking the misery and distress beneath her thin veneer of bravado, he would resign. If his judgment was that bad, he didn't have any business putting the rest of the team at risk. "Only if you object to women on the run hiding out here. I shouldn't have lied on my application, but the truth is, I don't have any experience or references. No one in Middletown—or even the US—knows me. And I've never worked a day in my life. Well, until today."

Now, that Tavish believed.

"The facts are that I'm a woman in dire need of an income. A place to stay. A way to build a life on my own."

"See, I told you someone would have to be desperate to take this job," Nolan teased, though his wisecrack fell flat. Most of the other agents were too busy absorbing every nuance of Karolena's delivery to make their own assessment of her sincerity. They couldn't help themselves. It was a survival instinct.

Tavish understood the hazard of coming to the wrong conclusion better than most.

"Are you kidding?" Karolena shook her head at him. "James offered a generous salary in addition to room and board. Plus built-in security. For that, I'd clean every inch of this place with my toothbrush, including the toilets."

"What kind of bawbag is after you?" Tavish couldn't suppress his curiosity a moment longer.

"My husband. He's...a very bad man." Karolena pinched the bridge of her nose.

She was *married*? Legend's head whipped toward her at that revelation.

"I don't plan to go back to him." She looked up at Legend as she turned stony again. "Not ever. I'd kill myself before I let him take me."

"Hey, no one here is going to force you to be with someone who hurts you," James cut in before Tavish could lose control of the emotions warring within him. Rage that she'd slept with them without divulging her relationship status, and a foolish urge to stand between her and whatever was chasing her despite her apparent lack of respect for full disclosure.

Their adorable manager was definitely the good cop to Jordan's bad cop. And James's compassionate approach seemed to work.

Karolena's eyes watered, though she looked up and away for several moments to keep her tears from falling. "Thank you, but you have no idea what I'm dealing with. I'm not talking about some working class guy who has too many drinks at the local bar and comes home to smack me around."

Which would be horrible enough, Tavish figured. What the hell was going on?

"We can handle it." Jordan spoke with such confidence while the rest of the Shields nodded in agreement, that she retuned her gaze to him, hopeful. So he continued. "This firm has a lot of experience. Some of us are ex-military. Others have worked for government agencies, and a few learned to fight in the streets. We're a lot more than our sign outside would have you believe. What kind of trouble are you in?"

Karolena looked from Jordan to Legend, then Tavish. She drummed her now uneven nails on the table as she considered her very limited options.

"You're going to think I'm crazy." She shook her head as if to herself. "It doesn't seem real, even to me, and I've lived it for more than ten years."

"It's important that you're honest with us now." Tavish tried not to growl. "We can help you, but only if you don't try to play us."

Though he didn't threaten her, she seemed to understand what he left unsaid. It wouldn't end well for her if she didn't come clean.

"Vladimir is the *pakhan* of one of the most powerful groups in the OPG. I guess here you would call that the Russian mafia, and he's a boss. My father sold me to that bastard when I was sixteen so he could pay to send my mom to a private nursing home after she suffered a brain aneurysm. He promised—and I honestly think he believed—I'd be treated like a queen. Instead I've been a possession, even if a prized one...at least to outside observers. One to hoard so no one steals it and one you can break in a fit of rage if you choose, simply because it's yours."

Ruby's fingers flew over her keyboard, and within moments, she displayed a photo on the giant curved screen of their command center.

Holy shit. If Tavish had thought Karolena was gorgeous in her causal clothes and messy bun, she stunned in the backless navy dress that hugged her subtle curves. Its crisscrossed straps stood in stark contrast to her porcelain skin. Long platinum hair fell in waves over her bare shoulders. Diamonds dripped from her ears and ringed her neck like a gleaming collar—which he supposed it had been—bringing out the frosty blue of her eyes.

Her fingers rested on the forearm of a man in an impeccably tailored suit, with a sharp nose, and a don't-fuck-with-me air. His hand pressed on top of hers, trapping it there while making it look like he returned an affection Tavish was certain she didn't actually feel. The practiced smile on her bright red lips didn't extend anywhere near her eyes and her expression was lifeless compared to how she'd looked when she'd unraveled around him.

At the sight of her past, Karolena recoiled. She slammed into the side of his arm as she turned away from the image of her husband. No, her captor, assuming what she was telling them was legit. He glanced at Ruby for a shred of reassurance and she nodded. Tavish wasn't sure if he should be glad or outraged that so far Karolena's story checked. Knowing she'd been mistreated was even harder to bear than the possibility she was a spy.

Though…there was still a chance that both were accurate.

It took a moment for him to notice the headline above the image, which appeared to be from some kind of gossip rag. It read *The Ice Princess Returns*.

"The Ice Princess?" Legend mumbled.

"It's awful, I know." Karolena shook her head. "There were a lot of times I was required to be on display by his side for public events. It was a respect thing. A big deal to him. I could only suffer through it by detaching myself from the surreal experience of being the envy of many women while hating every moment of my existence. I guess people thought that made me a good match for Vladimir. Cold, aloof, and devoid of emotion."

"You're anything but cold," Legend said quietly.

Tavish could have kicked Legend's ass when his kneejerk denial escaped. This was officially messy and it made him uneasy.

James's eyes widened as if he'd just now realized they hadn't wasted any time in taking Jordan at his word that as their boss he didn't give a fuck what they did while they were keeping her occupied. "I'm sorry that happened to you. Truly."

Karolena practically vibrated next to Tavish. She clutched her hands in her lap so hard he was sure it was a gesture she'd used often to wrangle her emotions out of sight while her face remained impassive. But was it because her past upset her or because she was making a last ditch attempt to mislead them?

It pissed him off how badly he wanted to accept her account.

"So you really expect us to believe that you finally managed to get out from under this dude, escaped the country, and wound up here, in the middle of Bumfuck Nowhere, right in our headquarters?" Tavish hated the odds of that. "Seems kind of convenient, huh?"

"I mean, not really. Right now it feels like a giant pain in my ass considering I'm trying to keep from drawing attention to myself. I was hoping you wouldn't be quite so thorough or...connected. Or likeable. Or hot." Karolena glared at him. "I need fewer complications in my life, not more."

Jordan silenced their bickering when he cut his gaze to Ruby. "On a scale of one to ten, how honest is she being?"

"Everything she says checks out with my research. There are photos of her wedding. She was clearly not of age to give consent based on her original birth certificate, though I found a falsified one filed with their marriage license. I've traced the payments in her father's name to the region's top long-term care facility. They don't come from his account at the local bank. He certainly doesn't have the means to afford it himself given he came from nothing and works as a clerk in a butcher shop. Case files from various, uh, *interested* international law enforcement agencies support Karolena's view of her husband and his status in the organization, which came to power due to brisk uranium trading back in the period following the fall of the Soviet Union. Today he and many of his officers are suspected in connection with crimes ranging from arms deals to drug smuggling to money laundering plus a high-end auto theft operation. It also seems his competitors have a habit of disappearing off the planet entirely. He's exactly the sort of asshole we're used to dealing with."

Karolena blinked a few times as if she hadn't expected the team to be that efficient. Or maybe she was processing Ruby's claim that they shoveled shit this deep most days.

Karolena had no idea what they were capable of.

But the way she kept peeking over her shoulder at the exit made it clear she was starting to get a clue and wondering how to extricate herself from the mess she'd fallen into. No amount of suds was going to clean this up.

"Your own fucking father did this to you?" James looked disgusted. "Don't tell my sister. Laurel will hunt him down and skin him alive."

For once, Nolan didn't make light of the situation. He scrubbed his hand over his face. "His sister is my girlfriend. Her and our boyfriend, Jace, are also victims of trafficking. We take it kind of personal."

James nodded, his features tight. "Our uncle did it to keep Laurel from accusing him of sexually assaulting her when she was a child. I would have done anything to protect her if I had known..."

"You were just a kid." Nolan squeezed James's hand.

James nodded. "But if I—*we*—can do something now. I want to. Please, Jordan. Can we help Karolena?"

She gasped. "Help me? No. I don't need anything except a way to make money—to live off of and to send home to my father since Vladimir is going to cut him off if he hasn't already—and people who won't ask a lot of questions."

Aarav snorted at that before setting his cup of tea on a coaster. "You're out of luck on that last part. Everyone's got their nose in everyone else's business around here."

"And there's no way in hell we're going to let someone get away with harming innocents if we can do something about it." Marcus toyed with the large diamond stud in his ear like he did when agitated, then turned to Jordan. "Right, boss?"

Karolena's voice got sharper then, her fear raising her pitch. "All I want is to be left alone."

Legend turned to her then and said softly, "Men like that don't stop just because you're gone. He'll try to find you. You'll live in constant fear. Even if he eventually gives up, he'll find a new toy and try to break her too. He's going to keep victimizing people. We can't look the other way and you wouldn't be safe staying here if we were the sort of people who could."

She took a few ragged breaths. "I'm not a selfish bitch. I would try to shut him down if it was possible. It's not. You don't understand the kind of power he has. I don't care how much training you have, you aren't going to be able to take him on. Plenty of people have tried. Governments even."

"Yeah, well, we don't have to play by their rules." Jordan smiled. "We're the people bureaucrats hire when they need something done that would cause far too much paperwork for official channels."

"Please don't ruin this one chance I have, however slim, to get away." Karolena gripped the arms of her chair so hard, Tavish half expected them to crack. She quivered as she fought dread and terror, refusing to let them overtake her.

Not only was she beautiful, but she was also brave and had stood strong—alone—for so long. He wished he could have told her she didn't have to be so tough anymore or at least not on her own. Assuming she wanted assistance from people not so different from the man she hated.

"What's your take?" Jordan looked to Tavish and Legend.

Maybe it was his own insecurities and the tenderness he already had for Karolena that made him lash out. Or maybe it was the bone-deep sympathy her story triggered in him. He couldn't afford to let his reflexive desire to protect or how deeply he was attracted to Karolena blind him to the truth. Not again.

"All I can say for certain is how she feels when she comes around me. That, I'm pretty damn sure, wasn't fake. The rest...hard to say."

Karolena bit her lip but didn't contradict him or bother to act like they hadn't gotten it on, but he'd bet anything she was holding on to that chair for two purposes now. One being to keep herself from smacking him across the face.

Kennedy grumbled, "Idiot."

Legend angled his chair toward them both and argued, "You can find out a lot about a person in a short amount of time if you spend it right. I believe her. And Tavish is acting like such an asshole because he does too, even if he doesn't like it."

Legend peeled Karolena's fingers from the arm of the chair closest to him and intertwined them with his own. She squeezed and held tight, as if he'd thrown her a lifeline. How long had she been drowning in panic and the impossibility of what she'd attempted by fleeing?

Karolena looked at Tavish, the full blast of her frozen blue eyes leveled on him.

He shrugged. "I can't decide what's worse. Either you're the world's greatest liar and none of that messed-up shit happened to you, or you're telling the truth and we're going to have to do something about it. Legend's right.

Even if it makes me the biggest idiot in the world, I'm glad you're nowhere near that bastard anymore."

"That makes two of us." Karolena seemed satisfied with his tentative support, as if it was more than she'd dared to hope for.

"So how *did* you escape anyway?" Legend asked.

"Before we get to that..." Jordan cleared his throat. "James has pointed out that it's pretty hypocritical to rip Karolena for lying to us when we haven't been entirely forthcoming about what it is we do here. If she's going to stay, she deserves to know what she's getting into."

"It can't be worse than what I left behind."

"Don't be so sure." Tavish figured he might as well do this fast and ruin whatever fragile shoot of affection that had sprouted between them in addition to the full blossom of attraction. "We're assassins."

"I don't know that word in English." She blinked at him. Could she not understand or did she not want to hear what he was telling her.

He spelled it out. "Killers for hire."

"Murderers?" Karolena's eyes went wide and she stood up so fast her chair rolled backward until it crashed into the wall.

"They prefer we not use the M word." James shrugged one shoulder. "But..."

"*Ubiytsy*?" Karolena reverted to Russian.

If Tavish had thought she was pale before, it was nothing compared to the bluish white cast her face took on as every drop of blood drained from it.

When none of them denied it, she bolted.

Too bad they weren't about to let her leave. Not now that they knew she was a victim. Ruby hit the panic button at her workstation. Metal shutters slid over the windows and exterior doors, which also meant they couldn't be opened from the inside.

Whether Karolena liked it or not, they would shelter her until they could deal with her ex-husband.

One way or another.

9

———

"We only kill bad guys!" Legend shouted as he chased after Karolena. It sounded absurd, even though it was true. He didn't blame her for running away from them—from him.

He slapped the leather back of Tavish's chair hard as he rushed past. The guy had issues, they all knew it. Especially when it came to trusting a lover. Legend figured it was the reason they'd ended up together. Tavish could have no doubts about Legend's loyalty since they'd saved each other's asses so many times throughout the years.

Because he loved the idiot, he'd dealt with Tavish's hang-ups and considered himself lucky to be with the guy, even if he was only a consolation prize to the other man.

Tavish could have eased Karolena into things if he'd used a damn molecule of tact. Instead, he'd relied on the shock value of blurting out a crass description of their profession to wedge some distance between them and her. Simply because they'd shared something beyond simple attraction. They'd fucked plenty of women together for him to be certain that what they'd done earlier was more than getting off. Of course, Tavish had responded by going chickenshit.

Karolena didn't deserve the fallout from Tavish's inability to trust a woman who turned him on.

Especially when she was already doing her best to separate herself from a man who operated outside the rules of polite society and had wielded that power to abuse her for her entire adult life...and then some.

Really, though, was there any good way to admit what they were? The things they did for money weren't so different from what Vladimir did. At least in the eyes of some.

Legend didn't regret taking down a single one of their targets. Doing so had saved lives and ended the suffering of so many more. Neither was he about to let Karolena fling herself into the path of whoever would be coming to find her.

That didn't mean he was an insensitive asshole.

By the time she'd reached the front doors, they were covered over by the blast-proof shutters. No amount of her pounding on them was going to budge either the glass or the slab of steel beyond it.

"Hey, Karolena." Legend slowed so that he wasn't charging at her while she was trapped. He spoke softly and held his hands out to his sides so she could see he wasn't trying to lunge for her either. "Give us a chance to explain."

She rounded on him, her platinum hair flaring out behind her. Her cheeks flushed even darker than when she'd ridden him so well upstairs. "I don't seem to have a choice! I never do."

Ah shit. They'd done to her exactly what Vladimir had

—locked her in, made her their prisoner—even if it was for her own good. He held his hand out to her, waiting for her to accept it. "I won't apologize for keeping you from harm, but I will ask Ruby to open the doors if you'll agree to hear us out. Take a few minutes to digest everything, calm down a bit, and let's see how we can work together. You need a concrete plan before you move, no matter what direction you go."

Karolena slapped his hand away. "I'd much rather be on my own. Let me out and I'll disappear again."

"You really believe he won't find you?" Legend shook his head. "I'm sorry to say I know guys like him. Losing you, especially if it looks like you chose to leave him, is a blow to his ego and to his reputation. He has to bring you back to show his men and his rivals that he's in control."

Karolena's shoulders slumped at that.

From behind him, in the direction of the conference room doorway, Ruby said softly, "He's right, you know. I'll open the doors. But you'd be foolish to walk through them."

One of Ruby's boyfriends, Ace, added, "You've tried Sweet & Spicy, the restaurant with the attached bakery on the corner, right?"

Karolena blinked as if she couldn't be bothered with something that insignificant at the moment. But Legend had a sick feeling he knew where the guy was going with his question. Dread knotted his guts.

Disarmed, she nodded. "I got a cup of coffee and a slice of baklava there before my interview."

Ace hummed. "I love Devra's desserts. Anyway, I went there this morning so I could bring Ruby and Liam breakfast in bed. They needed some fuel to make sure they could stay there a while with me."

Legend growled. "Get to the point."

"Our friends own the place. They mentioned that there were a couple of strangers with Russian accents in there yesterday. Didn't order anything or so much as take a peep in the pastry case. But asked if they'd seen a tall, thin blonde with bright blue eyes around town." Ace sighed. "Of course Devra and Morgan remembered you, since you'd been in only a couple hours before that. And last night, they spotted you at our party."

Karolena whimpered. With her back pressed to the doors, her legs gave out and she began to slide downward.

Legend rushed forward and scooped her up, hugging her to his chest. "We won't let them have you."

"Of course our friends played dumb. But..." Ace stepped aside so that Tavish could join them, a sheepish look on his face at least.

Legend and Tavish exchanged a worried glance over Karolena's head.

"So close. That was *too* close." She clutched Legend's shirt so tight her fists trembled. At least she wasn't shoving him away. It wasn't any major achievement to be considered a better alternative than the goons of the abusive fuck who'd made her life hell for a decade, but it was a start.

Tavish stroked her shoulder. "I'm sorry, Karolena. Can we bring you back into the command center to figure out what to do next?"

She went limp in Legend's hold as if every bit of fight had leached out of her. It scared him. Even when she'd been wrestling the mop, she'd never seemed defeated. "Yeah. Okay."

"Let me get the shutters." Ruby trotted to her computer. With a few taps, sunlight began spilling into the room once more. "Honestly, it's better if we don't draw too much attention to the building. Guys like that might wonder why a rinky-dink security service has sophisticated blast barriers."

As they approached their seats at the table, Tavish swiveled Legend's chair around and held it so that he could sink into it without having to let go of Karolena. He rocked her gently until her ragged breathing smoothed out a bit. When she lifted her cheek from his chest and realized the rest of the team was watching them intently, she pushed lightly on his ribs. He instantly set her in her place next to him.

"Thanks," she murmured.

He nodded, already missing the slight weight of her in his arms.

Tavish scooched his chair closer to her cautiously, as if expecting her to shove him away. But she didn't. Instead she sighed and rubbed her temples before saying to him, "Okay, so you're do-gooder assassins. Next you're going to tell me you're Robin Hood too."

Ruby bopped her head back and forth. "We did sort of have a recent foray into crypto and reassigning some funds..."

"Why? Why do I have this kind of luck?" Karolena dropped her head back. She was tall enough that it rested against the top of the chair while she stared up at the ceiling as if speaking to the universe. "I picked this town in the middle of fucking nowhere so there wouldn't be people doing...well, shit like this! It was supposed to be boring here."

"It's decent cover, we know." Sola beamed from her spot between Cash and Aarav. "Who would think to look for a group like ours here instead of New York or L.A. or even Miami, huh? Fortunately, there's plenty of land here for airfields. Jordan has a helicopter and a private jet. Our pilot, Aven, can fly us anywhere we need to go in a matter of hours. It's also great because it's super easy to spot newcomers and people who aren't from around here, like those two assholes hunting you."

Karolena groaned. "Don't remind me."

"So what would you like us to do about this situation?" Jordan wondered.

"You're asking me?" Karolena sat up straighter then, her head angled to one side as if gauging how serious he was.

"We shouldn't have forced you to stay." James winced. "It's just that you didn't have all the information you needed to make a sound decision and we couldn't risk you getting snatched from the parking lot while we hashed it out."

"Trust me. I give the kidnapping experience zero out of five stars. Do *not* recommend." Ruby reached for Liam's hand. He enfolded hers in his, reminding her that no one would ever be able to take her from him and Ace again.

"If you're comfortable with it, I'd recommend you continue to hang out with Legend and Tavish for a while. And if you want to share more, including how you got away and any details about Vladimir's operations that we could leverage with authorities, we'd be happy to see how we could help." Jordan had obviously been won over. Legend didn't blame the guy. Karolena was genuine. He could sense it and so could Tavish, even if he was afraid to rely on his instincts.

"I'm still not convinced you're going to be able to do anything, but if you're willing to listen...you're the best chance I have at getting away for good. The only one, really." Karolena took a moment to compose herself, and when she opened her eyes she was sitting up straight, meeting their gazes directly. She was a fighter.

Jordan steepled his fingers. "If nothing else, we should be able to exchange your information and cooperation for legitimate papers. I'm assuming you'd be deported if anyone looked too closely at yours."

Her throat flexed as she swallowed hard. "I don't know. You're probably right, though I hadn't thought about that. There's a lot I have no idea about. And yes, I couldn't have done this on my own. I had help with the documents and the circumstances that allowed me to make a run for it. Literally."

Legend tried to reassure her. "Fortunately, Jordan used to be an agent for ICE. They're the part of our government that handles this sort of stuff. He has connections. He helped Devra get out of some trouble once."

She nodded. "Okay. That's good. Thank you. I wish I could have been better prepared. Things happened fast once I'd made up my mind and it was never easy to ensure I was speaking privately with my friend."

Jordan pried a bit. "We'll need to know their name."

Karolena hesitated. "I don't want to trade my safety for his. It's important to me that anything I tell you isn't used against him and that every attempt to spare him will be made. Is that even possible?"

Tavish rubbed a hand down his beard, obviously thinking of how his own family and friends had been impacted by his choices. Their work wasn't some nine to five where the worst peril was a paper cut. There were real consequences to what they did. Karolena's friend could easily get caught in the crossfire.

Legend sighed. "We can't promise he won't get hurt,

Karolena. And you shouldn't believe us or anyone else who'd make such a bold claim. What we do is hazardous. And just because this dude helped you doesn't mean he's blameless. But we'll try our best."

That must have been good enough for Karolena. "Levin is pretty much the only true friend I've ever had."

Ruby zoomed in on the background of Karolena and Vladimir's photo. A man with golden eyes lurked on the fringes of the limelight. He had a way of holding his well-toned body that spoke of readiness to fight. Alert, he stood with his hands clasped in front of him as he scanned the crowd snapping photos of the power couple. "Levin Fedorov. Rumored to be the head of the security branch of Vladimir's operation."

"We call his position *Obshchak*, one of the two spies." Karolena nodded.

"I like this dude already." Knox spun his chair for a better look, planting his elbows on his knees as he leaned forward.

"He's essentially second in command only to Vladimir himself," Karolena informed them.

"And he had a soft spot for you?" Tavish asked, not in the least subtle.

"Quit that." Legend glared at his partner. Now wasn't the time to interject over misplaced jealousy. They needed to learn as much as they could from Karolena if they were going to have any shot at protecting her.

"He's always treated me like a little sister." Karolena's lips softened and curved upward a bit as she replayed some memory of the man. "In fact, that's what he calls me when no one else can hear. *Sestra*. It will break me if he gets into trouble because of what I'm telling you or how he helped me."

"To be fair, he's some high-ranking mafia bastard," Tavish grumbled. "Guaranteed anyone who's called a security officer in that organization has blood on his hands."

"You above all should know things aren't always black and white." Karolena shifted her focus to Tavish. "Sometimes extreme measures are justified. Aren't they?"

"Not when the end goal is to take a girl captive or steal a fancy car or sell guns to terrorists in order to profit. Nope." Tavish popped the P.

"Levin was born into this. His father was *obshchak* before him. He doesn't know anything else, any other way of being. Or he didn't until recently. About a year or two ago he started changing. I noticed it bit by bit. He started acknowledging me, talking to me while waiting for meetings with Vladimir. He often escorted me from social events after I'd made enough of an appearance to suit Vladimir and before he settled in for serious negotiations or whatever deals he would make under the guise of a cocktail party. Several times, Levin was there to clean me up after Vladimir had used me particularly harshly or taken out his anger over who knew what on me. He's cleaned my wounds and even stepped between us to keep me from getting worse punishment a few times. Never once did he make me feel ashamed and even convinced me, over time, that it wasn't my fault Vladimir never seemed pleased with me."

Legend stiffened, wishing there was something he could do to erase the remembered agony causing her voice to waver for a moment.

"So Levin convinced you to leave?" Kennedy asked, her fingers locked together as if to keep them still while imagining Karolena being beaten. Suffering always took a toll on their medic, and she'd seen plenty of it.

"He did." She swallowed as if even remembering scared her. "He said he could get papers, arrange a private flight, send me far away where I could start over. It sounded like a dream. So when I agreed, in theory, I didn't think he'd act so quickly. It was only a week later when he picked me up from a party at one of his brigadier's mansions. As soon as I got in the car, Levin handed me a backpack full of cash and said that when it was time, I should run. He gave me an address, and the name of the man who would meet me there and take me to a waiting jet."

She paused, taking several deep shaky breaths as if even now she wasn't sure they could pull it off.

Tavish cracked. He reached over and offered his hand, which she clasped before continuing. "I asked why he couldn't take me himself, or come with me, but he insisted he had to stay behind to divert Vladimir's attention. To throw him off the scent until I was off the ground and out of reach. It seemed like there was something else but he never had a chance to say what. Before I was ready, he rear-ended a car in downtown traffic, blocking the street. Not just a fender bender either. I think he was hurt pretty bad, maybe broke his leg. He screamed at me to run. To flee while there was a distraction and a reason he could give Vladimir for how I got loose. I think he planned to blame it on another gang, but I'm not sure."

Karolena rubbed her upper arm, which had been obscured by her T-shirt even while they were fucking. Was she injured? Had they aggravated any wounds while they were screwing around? She lifted the edge of the cotton to reveal a scabbed over gash that could probably have used stitches and would definitely leave a scar.

Legend groaned.

"I climbed out the smashed window, grabbed the backpack, and ran as fast as I could for as long as I could away from the sirens, then took a taxi to the spot Levin had arranged. I don't remember much after getting on the plane. I was in shock, pretty sure. And next thing I knew, I was getting on a bus heading for a town I'd never heard of and hoped no one else in Russia had either."

"Damn, Karolena." James sank deeper into his chair. "That must have been terrifying."

"It still is." She didn't bother to lie anymore. "It's weird out here. Overwhelming. Deciding what clothes I'm going to buy, or what to have for breakfast, or where to go... Honestly, I don't really like being by myself. I'm not used to it, and so when James said I could stay here—"

Her voice broke and she took a minute to get herself together again. Legend rested his hand on her knee. She seemed to appreciate his support, resting her head on his shoulder for a moment.

"I'm worried for Levin. I haven't had a friend since I went to live with Vladimir, which is part of what finally made me realize how wrong my life was." She looked to Jordan. "Can you help him too? He said he didn't want to wreck my chances, but I suspect there's something else to it."

"Honestly, this is what we do." Jordan nodded slowly. "We look for entry points, connections that could undermine an entire organization. This lead could be what puts a stop to this for good. Then you—and your friend, if he agrees to facilitate the mission—could start fresh. You wouldn't have to worry constantly about your past catching up with you. It would be a permanent solution."

Karolena looked to Legend. He doubled down. "We're good at what we do, I swear. With reliable intel and the backing—official or not—of international law enforcement, we're capable of pulling this off. Vladimir won't be able to bug you, and he'll never be able to do what he's done to you to anyone else either."

"Plus, if you stay with us, we'll take real good care of you." Tavish couldn't help but reduce the genuine emotion swirling between Legend and Karolena to something crude. His tone made it obvious he was referring to what they'd done earlier. He coped by downplaying what they'd done, which irritated Legend. Of course Karolena didn't understand.

"Not exactly subtle, are you? Was this your plan from the start?" She narrowed her eyes at Legend, then cut her stare to Tavish. "Did you fuck me to make it more likely I would agree to this?"

The murmurs around the boardroom table made it clear their friends were settling some bets. Had they expected the partners to act so fast? Legend hadn't, but he wasn't mad about it either. Unless jumping into a physical relationship so soon had fucked things up between the three of them for the long run, because their explosive session earlier had proved to him that even several stellar orgasms weren't going to be enough to satisfy his appetite for Karolena and sharing her with Tavish.

Lost in thought, Legend didn't deny Karolena's assumptions fast enough. She rounded on him. "Does Jordan pay you extra when you have to sleep with an informant to soften them up?"

Ah damn, she had been so soft. And warm. And wet.

He shook his head. "Shit, no."

"What he means is the idea was all theirs," James clarified, helping the partners pull their boots out of their mouths. "And purely for recreational purposes. No one is going to judge you for having a good time around here."

"See, that's what we told you before." Legend was going to have to figure out how to communicate better. With Karolena, sure, and also with Tavish. He'd let things drag on too long while the other man licked his wounds.

Karolena read the room, then nodded slowly, as if it was nearly impossible for her to believe them.

"Here's what we're going to do." Jordan returned to business mode. He paused for James, who flipped open his fancy-ass planner and color-coordinated pens to take notes. "I'm going to call some people and tell them about this unique opportunity we have. I'll find out what their level of interest is in intervening. In the meantime, Ruby is going to divide the dossiers of information I'm sure she's been downloading this entire time and assign them to you all to comb through. Let's identify any gaps and figure out what Karolena might know that could be valuable to putting together a plan of attack."

"And us?" Legend asked, hoping he knew the answer.

"I'm not even going to try to keep you three apart." Jordan rolled his eyes. "Stay with her. It's not a hardship, is it?"

Tavish muttered, "It will be if I do something dumb."

"Like what?" Karolena asked him sharply.

Legend wondered the same thing. Sleeping with her hadn't seemed to bother Tavish. No, it was putting faith in Karolena or allowing himself to experience affection for her in addition to lust that was freaking him out. And he was too fucking petrified to be as gutsy as her and admit his anxieties out loud.

Instead, he cracked a joke.

"I'm getting too old for screwing on every flat surface. Next time I'm going to need a bed, or at least the carpet instead of the table."

"Remind me never to accept a dinner invitation from you two," James teased.

"Don't worry, I'll clean it. Again." Karolena crossed her arms. "Seems like I'm going to have a lot of free time."

"Way to ruin it for us both." Legend glared and the rest of the Shields chuckled. It had been a hell of a lot more amusing to him when the other trios were struggling to figure their shit out.

If he wasn't fighting Tavish and his insecurities, they might be able to create something lasting together. How the hell was he going to prove to both Tavish and Karolena that if they entrusted more than simply their bodies to him, he would take care of them like the rest of the people who'd let them down should have too?

Legend figured his assignment was the most difficult of all.

"Okay, let's get to work." Jordan pushed back from the table and stood. "One more thing..."

Legend knew he was going to hate whatever it was his boss had saved for last.

"Someone go over to Sweet & Spicy. Tell Morgan and Devra that if those guys come back, they should pass along a message. Let them know that if the woman they're looking for is in Middletown, they're only going to find her if they send Levin in person for a meeting."

"Son of a bitch." Tavish groaned.

"I don't like that. At all." Legend agreed with his

partner's assessment of exactly how terrible a scheme that was. Though really, those assholes had tracked her that far. It wasn't going to be long before they realized where she was holed up. Did he hate it more because he didn't want her in any more danger, or because he wanted her to stay away from the one man in her past she gave a shit about?

Maybe he wasn't much better than Tavish after all.

"I'm on that. I'll grab everyone lunch while I'm there. Text me your orders." James waggled his phone. "And soon enough, Karolena's friend will be here so we can figure out how to stop these assholes for good."

Karolena smiled for the first time since she'd admired the results of her labor in their apartment earlier. "Thank you. Really. I don't care so much about myself. I mean, I do, but...if that's all it was, it would be one thing. If I could stop this from happening to anyone else, ever again, that would make everything I've gone through mean something. The suffering would be worth it."

Legend recognized the spark in her eyes. The drive to set things to rights inspired her. Gave her purpose. And in that moment, he fell for her a little bit, because he held a twin flame deep in his soul.

It was then he realized James was going to be bummed because Karolena had never been destined to be their housekeeper. He didn't know exactly how or in what capacity yet, but he was sure she was going to be a Shield and protect others the way no one had done for her.

10

Karolena's head spun as she reentered Tavish and Legend's apartment. So much had changed.

After years of stagnation, things kept evolving before she could adjust to the previous iteration of what her life had become. Though she would never have admitted it out loud, it sort of stressed her out to make her own decisions about every aspect of her new existence.

Overwhelmed, she wandered to the windows again, sinking onto the floor, her legs folded and tucked beneath her. She stared out at the clouds floating past as she reflected on that harried flight into darkness and how she'd awoken into the dawn as her plane had touched down. The bus ride across an unfamiliar land, her stark hotel room, shopping in a department store without an escort, interviewing and landing a job, moving in, then hooking up with the pair of nice guys—who'd turned out to be well-meaning executioners—and the possibility of a future where she could do something more than look pretty and dread every moment.

It was a lot to process.

She hugged her abdomen and swayed as she counted the cars that passed on the streets below, looking like toys from her perch on the fifth floor. "Please don't stand there and gawk at me like that."

"Huh?" Tavish tried to play dumb.

"I can see your reflection in the tinting." She shook her head. "Shouldn't a superspy know that?"

Despite her warning, he exchanged another worried stare with Legend.

"You okay, Karolena?" Legend shuffled to her side and crouched down. "Want something to eat? A drink? I have a pitcher of iced tea leftover from the party last night."

She perked up at that. "The plain kind or the Long Island kind?"

"Regular. I know you said you don't drink alcohol." He smiled gently, his face growing even more handsome. As much as she wished it didn't, his kindness and attentiveness reassured her some.

"I'd like to start now, please."

Tavish headed straight for the kitchen. "I can make it into the other sort, no problem."

"How can I help?" Legend asked.

"Just...sit quietly with me, if you don't mind?" Karolena needed to think. "You know, as nice as this place is, it could really use some balconies to take advantage of this view. The windows don't even open. I wish I could breathe some fresh air."

"Security risk." Legend grimaced as if he despised reminding her of their occupation.

"I wish there wasn't a need for caution."

"The world sucks sometimes. I'm sorry." Was he apologizing for evil in general, for his role in fighting it, or for entangling her in more of it right when she'd thought she'd left it behind for good? Of course that presumption hadn't been correct, but it had felt like a victory until she'd faced reality.

For a while, they simply sat there side-by-side, Legend with his arms looped over his knees. She watched birds soaring above the treetops in the distance, oblivious to the problems of everyone beneath them. She had never wanted to fly so much as at that moment.

"Here, let's pretend."

Before she could ask Legend what he meant, he snagged a couple beanbags and throw pillows from in front of the giant TV connected to the gaming system she'd carefully dusted earlier. He plopped them on the floor, then disappeared down the hallway toward his bedroom before returning with an oscillating fan on a pole stand. He placed it in the corner where the windows met the wall and turned it on. A breeze began drying the sheen of cold sweat that had broken out on her skin when she realized Vladimir's men were right on her heels. Then he set the high-backed, slatted dining room chairs in a rectangle around her so they gave the impression of a railing.

For bonus points, he added a couple of their houseplants to the perimeter of the space he'd created. If she squinted, she might believe she was lounging on a balcony instead of their dining room floor. She half-closed her eyes, letting the cool air wash over her. Karolena studied the world passing by outside as if today was perfectly normal instead of a whole new beginning.

Legend vaulted over a chair, making it seem as inconsequential as a threshold and landed lightly beside her. He was capable of so much more than she'd given him credit for, even after he'd infused her with pleasure that was the stuff of her fantasies. He held out his hand, and when she took it, he pulled her up just enough to help her off the floor into the beanbag.

She practically moaned as she curled up in the fuzzy ball, which felt like it was giving her a full body hug. Legend smiled, then took a seat in the one next to her. It was only another minute or two before Tavish returned. "Oh, are we having a picnic?"

Legend peered over his shoulder, then raised his arm to accept the tray Tavish handed him before climbing over the faux-railing himself. Of course, from where they were sitting, that gave her and Legend a peek up his kilt. He still wasn't wearing underwear. The view was even more memorable than the scenery out of the windows.

"Damn. Watch where you're flashing those things," Legend muttered as he set the platter on the floor in between them.

Tavish cracked up as he stretched out on the ground opposite the refreshments from Legend and Karolena. He rolled onto his side on a few of the pillows, then used one bent arm to prop his head up. "I brought some of those baby sandwiches and charcuterie stuff they had last night too. You don't want to drink this too fast or on an empty stomach."

He handed her the frosty glass full of spiked tea with a pretty white-and-blue striped paper straw.

Before Karolena could protest that she wasn't hungry, her watering mouth argued otherwise. She plucked a sandwich from the tray and inhaled it in three bites before drawing on her drink.

When she sputtered, then coughed from behind her

splayed hand, Legend glared at Tavish. "How strong did you make that?"

"Not half as potent as I'd pour it for you. Settle down, Papa Bear." Tavish rolled to his back, then turned his head away from them, taking some solace of his own from the pretty view.

As frustrated as Karolena had been with him earlier, she felt bad. "It's great. Thank you."

Legend cleared his throat as he reached for a slice of apple and a piece of some sort of cured meat. "Yeah, thanks."

The combination of the breeze that kept her from feeling trapped, and the chairs, which prevented her from feeling too exposed, plus the presence of the guys keeping her company without demands, and the food filling her belly while the drink loosened her muscles—including her tongue—all worked together, inspiring her to pry. "Tavish, what's your problem?"

He faced her again at that. "I'm just lying here."

"Now." She took another long sip. "Downstairs you were hostile, and I don't think I did anything to deserve that from you."

Karolena had had enough of keeping her opinions under wraps. Or letting others turn her into collateral damage because of their foul moods. She'd become an expert in sensing people's emotions since she'd often had to dodge Vladimir's bad moods. Trauma was good for something anyway.

Legend responded before Tavish could. "He's afraid of you. Fucking terrified, actually."

The way Tavish's fingers squashed an unfortunate piece of cheese before he popped it into his mouth made her think that as ludicrous as it sounded, Legend might actually be right.

"Me? Why?" Her eyes widened. No one had ever been scared of her and never needed to be either.

When Legend opened his mouth, Tavish frowned. "I can speak for myself."

"Yeah, but will you?" Legend lifted one shoulder. "She's shared hard stuff today. You owe her the same respect. Don't make some dumb excuse, or worse, a joke. Be honest."

Tavish glanced in the direction of the refrigerator before he crumbled inward, placing a cracker he'd been about to eat back on the tray as if he'd lost his appetite.

"Does it have to do with your family? And that beautiful bride?" Karolena held her glass out to him, but he shook his head.

"We don't drink on assignment, but thanks." He scrunched his eyes closed like the photo wasn't burned into his memory, then nodded. "My date to that wedding —my brother's, by the way—blamed my new sister-in-law for a ruling she'd made while serving in the College of Justice. So she got close to me, slept with me, made me believe we were in love, then set off a pipe bomb in the middle of their reception. She slaughtered them on the happiest day of their lives. If she hadn't gone out with the bang, along with most of my family and friends, I don't know what I would have done to her. But I wonder every day why it wasn't me who paid the price for being so stupid."

Karolena splashed some of her tea over the rim of her cup as she clunked it onto the tray, then held her arms out, open, to Tavish. No one deserved to carry a burden that heavy on their own.

"I don't know how many times I've said it...and I know this one won't be the time that convinces you...but it wasn't your fault, Tavish. You were a naive college kid. You didn't have any of the training you do now and what happened still wouldn't have been on you if you had." Legend scrubbed his hand over his face. "I wish I could make you see that you're not to blame."

It took five seconds—or maybe ten—but Karolena didn't budge.

Eventually, Tavish rose from the floor and plucked her out of the beanbag. He took her place in it and hugged her tight to him as his breathing sawed in her ear. She'd never realized how effective a comforting embrace could be, but holding him and being held in return did something to her insides.

Or at least she thought it was that and not his special tea.

Maybe it was both.

"Would you say I'm responsible for the things Vladimir did to me? Or even to others when I watched and couldn't stop him?" she whispered in his ear, legitimately worried about his censure.

"Of course not." He stroked one hand through her hair as he rested their foreheads together and looked straight into her eyes. "He's a monster."

"So was she."

Legend spilled from his beanbag and knelt beside them, kissing each of them on their cheek. "You're so resilient, both of you."

"Am I, though?" Tavish looked at them, his emerald eyes swimming a bit. "I've wounded you, Legend. I know that. And I can't seem to stop. Karolena, too. My ability to trust is broken."

"So is mine," she murmured. "I couldn't even take my clothes off before, never mind have sex in a bed, or let you be on top, or even share a simple kiss. You're not the only one here who's fucked up."

"It's been like five minutes since you've been free and had a chance to start healing. I've had years to process this shit and I've hardly made any progress." Tavish clutched her. For whose sake, she wasn't sure, but she liked it.

"So that's how you came to Shields? You were trying to keep anyone else from ever having to go through what you did." Karolena stroked down the side of his face and cupped his cheek, his beard pressing into the heel of her hand.

"Yeah. I kind of went vigilante for a while, but I ran into Legend when he was on a mission with the military —secret ops shit—and we stuck together. I was a 'consultant' on a bunch of jobs for a division that doesn't exist on paper. Not too long ago, Jordan recruited us. When we learned the purpose of Shields and were offered the chance to formally become partners, we were in. Best thing that ever happened to me, truly. The team here understands me. Accepts me, and all my quirks."

Karolena couldn't believe she wasn't appalled, but instead she found it was a turn-on. To think of them against the worst parts of the world, trying to make a difference. Kicking ass and sharing women when they needed to relax. They loved as intensely as they fought. They were everything she'd dreamed of and never believed existed—men who vowed to do the right thing, no matter the cost. Sure, they had their own code of ethics and integrity, but it wasn't based on benefiting themselves.

She peeked up at Legend, who was studying her and Tavish entwined as if the sight was as soothing to him as their respite on the "balcony" was to her. "And you? Why'd you leave the military?"

"To be with Tavish." His blunt response held a lot of weight. Unlike her and Tavish, Legend wasn't afraid to be honest with himself or with them.

Against her thigh, Tavish's cock responded to the smolder in his partner's stare. She ignored it...for the moment.

"Come on. You were eager to ditch the rules and go rogue. I know you were." Tavish deflected a bit when the intensity of Legend's attention was too much to bear.

"That too." Legend's mouth kicked up on one side. "I enjoy addressing issues we come across without sawing through a mile of red tape first. Shields are more direct and we can fix a lot problems because of it."

"I'm jealous that you two have a purpose." She sighed and snuggled up against Tavish, their talk and her drink making his welcoming hold impossible to resist. "Don't tell James, but...I *hate* cleaning."

Tavish howled with laughter, bouncing her on his chest. "That is not a secret."

"I admit, I've been spoiled and gotten used to finer things. Fancy food, nice clothes, stuff like that. But I want to earn them myself. Do you think Jordan would let me help with other cases? Could I be trained to do something useful?"

"Why don't we start with self-defense lessons?" Legend didn't answer her directly, probably because Tavish tensed up. She would give him the benefit of the doubt and assume it was because he was alarmed by the possibility of losing anyone else in his life, not because he didn't like the thought of working with her. "You should know how to protect yourself in case we're ever caught with our pants...or kilt...down."

Karolena nodded. "That's a great idea. It can wait until tomorrow, though. Right?"

"Yeah." Tavish adjusted so they sank deeper into the beanbag. "I think we've taken enough of a beating today. Reliving this shit isn't easy. I'm so sorry you had to go through all that, Karolena. Especially the stuff with your dad."

She shrugged. "That's the easiest to understand, really. Everyone has priorities and my mother is his. He adores her. Made sure to take her to the ballet for every show, even when they could hardly afford it. And when I came along, he gave his season ticket to me so I could watch the ballerinas. I would dance around the house and they would clap so loud. But when she...got sick...all he could focus on was how to take care of her. Hard to fault him for that."

"I suspect your mom would if she knew what he did, especially in her name." Legend glowered. "If she was to wake up, your dad would be in for a hell of a shock."

"Well, she's not going to, so..." Karolena shrugged. "Family is who you choose. I've already learned that much from coming here. I've never had anyone I wanted to pick for my team before. Except Levin. And only lately."

"I don't understand how you can be so forgiving." Tavish studied her as if she was as mythical as the Loch Ness monster instead of too tired to maintain the wrath necessary to abhor someone forever. "I'm stuck. Angry at myself every day. Part of my soul is black and dead and I don't know if it will ever come back to life. Hell, I've worn a damn kilt every day since they died. I used to only do that on special occasions, to make my granny happy, but I guess I feel closer to them when I do. A way to honor them and never forget."

"There's nothing wrong with that." Legend put his hand on Tavish's shoulder.

"I think it's sweet." Karolena braced her palms on his chest and separated them a bit so she could stare directly into his eyes. She hadn't thought she'd ever be ready to share something so intimate with someone, but Tavish had bared parts to her that she was sure saw less light of day than the bits beneath his kilt. So she rewarded him by leaning in and pressing her lips to his.

It was her first real kiss. And maybe his too. Or at least in a while.

Because pure, honest emotion instantly linked them as their mouths soothed each other. He sipped from her with far more caution than she'd used when gulping her tea, savoring each taste as if he knew precisely how much it meant that she was willing to partake in this act with him. He flicked his tongue against the seam of her lips and she moaned, which permitted him inside just a bit.

Wonder flowed through her. She'd never suspected a basic action could move her so much.

Legend cleared his throat. "Before you two get too carried away..."

Karolena peered up at him. What was he trying to say? It seemed important.

"Too late." Tavish nudged her chin so that she focused on him again and kept kissing.

At least until Karolena insisted her brain engage long enough to see what was bothering Legend. "Hmm?"

He snapped her out of the pleasant daze Tavish was putting her in when he asked, point blank, "Why'd you fuck us? After everything you've been through, I'm struggling with that some."

"Are you seriously complaining?" Tavish reached over with his foot and shoved Legend's shin. "Quit thinking and go with it."

Karolena wished it was that easy, but she could see he wasn't about to let it go. Talking could only lead to more drama. More entanglements. And she had no desire for that. All she sought was the bliss and pleasure-blanked mind that came from spending time between him and Tavish.

"I need to know." Legend repeated, "Why'd you fuck us?"

Karolena didn't intend to waste even one precious second they could spend enjoying each other instead of arguing, so she cut to the chase. "To see if I could feel anything when I never had before, except maybe disgust."

"You'd have to be dead not to feel the big guy over there. And we're not into necro." Tavish wrinkled his nose, making her chuckle.

"Do not encourage him. Please." Legend shoved Tavish back. "So, uh, did you?"

If she was smart, she'd let Legend's question frighten her away. Because the truth was, she'd felt so much that she was terrified nothing could top it. Or that she could become too attached to the first two men she met after leaving her prison.

But she could see it, etched into the worry lines on his forehead and around his eyes. Legend didn't understand how profoundly he'd moved her earlier or...worse...how badly his partner needed him too.

She flicked her gaze to Tavish, who was puzzled. Was he oblivious to the impact his own trauma had on his partner? Didn't he see Legend desperately required reassurance that he was more to the other man than a good time?

"Did you feel something, I mean." Legend cleared his throat, then admitted, "Because I did."

She reached over and squeezed his forearm. "Of course I did. Something more potent than I expected, and addictive too. Something I don't ever want to be deprived of again now that I know it exists."

"Does that mean we're going to fuck again?" Tavish asked with a wry smile.

"No." Legend seemed unwilling to let him blow it off, this chemistry they had together.

"We're not?" Karolena tried not to be disappointed.

"What we're going to do is more serious than that. We don't have to give it a label, but I refuse to let him pretend it's not meaningful beyond temporary, physical relief. Not anymore." Legend looked at Tavish. Then at Karolena. "Agreed?"

She nodded.

Tavish hesitated for a few heartbeats, then drummed up the courage to do the same.

11

Tavish might have panicked and tried to distract Legend from serious shit, like he usually did, with an epic blow job or by drilling him into the floor. Except Karolena was there. He suspected she wasn't going to let him get away with cheap tactics like that anymore. Not when she'd been used by several people who were supposed to care for her.

Those days were over. If Tavish wanted Legend, and Karolena too, he was going to have to be upfront about why. It wasn't only because they were gorgeous and desirable—her beauty to Legend's beast.

So he forced himself to meet their expectations so he deserved what they were willing to give him in return. With Karolena still in his lap, he stretched out one arm and curled his left hand around the back of Legend's neck, using the firm but careful grip to draw the bigger guy to them.

The position gave Karolena a front row seat to their spectacle. So he slammed his mouth over Legend's. Their kiss was nothing like the sweet silk of the one he'd shared with Karolena. It was aggressive and raw. Pure passion. Just what he needed to vent the anxiety and grief that assaulted him when he revisited his past. Tavish groaned and nipped at Legend's lower lip, holding it between his teeth as he pulled away a bit, only releasing the other man when he grunted.

"Damn," Karolena whispered reverently. "Don't make fun of me, but I had no idea guys really did that with each other. Or that it would be so hot if they did."

Tavish cut his stare to her incredulously, but he didn't stop.

"It's not exactly accepted in my country and especially in the mafia, or at least that's what I was always told. I'm starting to think a lot of what I thought I knew about the world is bullshit." She reached up and traced the juncture of their lips, her finger getting nipped in the process.

Karolena yelped and yanked her slender finger back, popping it into her own mouth for a moment. With her touch withdrawn, Tavish could concentrate on making out with Legend. The guy never got enough of this. He ate up affection and Tavish was sure it was because Tavish doled out so little.

It wasn't Legend's fault Tavish had been broken following his betrayal, and still Legend had been so damn patient.

Tavish didn't intend to make him wait anymore. He thrust his tongue into Legend's mouth and moaned when the other guy immediately began to suck on it, taking everything he gave and then some.

"Do you two want some privacy?" Karolena's timid question penetrated Tavish's guilty conscience.

Rather than answer, he wrapped his right arm around her waist and kept her close. Trying not to be greedy as fuck, he broke his lip lock with Legend, then guided the other man to Karolena instead.

She balked, craning her neck away. "I don't want a pity kiss. I can see you two have a real bond and I won't come between you."

"What makes you think sharing him with you will damage our connection?" Tavish rubbed his nose on her cheek. "I promise you, it only makes it stronger."

"Oh, uh. I guess because I'm not sure how it works. I've never had anything significant with someone before, never mind two different people."

"Well, you do now." Tavish stole one tiny taste of sunshine, lemon, and vodka from her lips. She leaned into him before he pressed on the nape of Legend's neck, encouraging his lover to take his place. If nothing else, he could be generous and give Legend more than his fair share of their playmate.

Besides, watching them go at it wasn't a hardship.

Legend was oversized but far gentler than Tavish. Controlled and restrained. So careful that Tavish was sure he'd always been conscious of how easy it would be for him to accidentally injure one of his partners—something he'd never do. For someone who kicked ass for a living, and had never hesitated to do so in the field, it was almost comical but ultimately so damn endearing that Tavish melted inside with every swipe of Legend's lips over Karolena's.

He elicited sighs from her, his thumbs stroking her cheekbones as he thanked her for allowing them to give her the pleasure of their kisses. Only hours before, she hadn't been willing to be so vulnerable with them. And neither man was oblivious to the honor she was bestowing on them by doing so then.

After a while, Karolena practically vibrated in Tavish's arms, her ass pressing against him as she swayed in time to the pace Legend set. And when he paused to catch his breath, Tavish jumped in, swapping places and keeping Karolena in the zone.

Their advance was painfully slow and steeped in casual intimacy. He could honestly say it had been a long time since he'd enjoyed a trip to first base so much. Probably because he knew how significant it was to both her and Legend to share this with each other.

So they kept at it for a long time, Legend and Tavish trading off, tasting each other on her lips.

And when she gasped then drew in several deep lungfuls of air, they gave her a break and feasted on each other again.

"Damn." She panted as she rested her head on Tavish's shoulder and studied them up close. "I can't believe I lost so much time. I could have been doing this for an entire decade already. Actually enjoying myself and building something real and lasting. What a fucking waste."

"I'm guilty too," Tavish admitted both to them and himself. "I walled myself off after..."

"So we'll start now. Together." Legend's tone was matter-of-fact. As if it only made sense. And somehow, although it had happened in a flash, it did.

Maybe all these years they'd simply been waiting for the right catalyst to trigger this explosion of passion blended with emotion. A cocktail so perfectly mixed, Tavish was already drunk off it and thirsty for far more than was wise.

Understandably, Karolena needed the most convincing. He couldn't imagine how mind-boggling it was for her and how surreal it must seem. "Will we?

Obviously, you guys sleep with more than one person. Does that mean you'll see other women—or men—too?"

"Would you care if we did?" It was a purely theoretical question, but Tavish wondered if she was as invested as they already were.

"Yeah. I think so." Karolena bit her lip, which Legend soothed with another lingering kiss.

"Don't worry. That's not how this works for us," he promised her.

"It scarred me when Vladimir slept around on me and I didn't even like that bastard." Karolena closed her eyes briefly. "How fucked up is that?"

"Not at all. You have a right to expect your partners to respect whatever boundaries you set together. James and his spouses have polyamorous relationships with their friends in the Powertools crew. It works for them and that's awesome." Legend tucked a strand of hair behind her ear.

"But it's equally important for you to be honest, mostly with yourself, about what it's going to take to make you happy. All the trios here at Shields are committed threesomes." Tavish hoped she approved. "Just because we like to share our women and indulge in some sword crossing while we're at it doesn't mean we're incapable of being faithful."

"We're hoping to find the right person to fit with us and make us a unit." Legend put it out there in the open. It was a dream they'd been too afraid would never come true to speak of it so plainly before. Not even to each other.

But it was starting to seem possible, so Tavish didn't bother denying it.

"We're nothing like your ex," Legend insisted. "The

difference is respect. We're looking for someone to be ours, someone we can give ourselves to completely."

Karolena nodded. "I don't know if I'm that person, but as long as I know that's your goal, I'm less afraid. Or maybe more in some sick way."

"What's that mean?" Tavish pressed a kiss to her forehead.

"I'm worried I could get really used to this—you two, the way you make me feel, safety, having choices, your friends, being spoiled, and especially this place. It's fancy and full of people pursuing their passions. A life I've always fantasized about with none of the drawbacks of my previous one. A means of keeping some of those same privileges I had before but at a cost I am willing to pay. Now that I've seen what it could be like, I don't want to lose it before I've ever really had it."

"Then let's make the most of every minute we have. In our line of work, that's really the best you can hope for." Tavish didn't want her to have any misconceptions. The expected lifespan of an agent was far shorter than that of an average Joe. Workplace mishaps were usually more serious than a finger mashed in a stapler.

Karolena reached for her mostly forgotten glass and took a couple solid swigs. Then she nodded. The time for kissing had passed. All of them required something stronger.

"Is it okay to undress you this time?" Tavish ran his finger along the neckline of her T-shirt, dipping into the point of the V and tugging downward to display the upper swells of her pert breasts.

Karolena considered his request for a few heartbeats, which thumped in the base of his cock. "As long as you go first."

That was not a problem. Hell, he loathed wearing clothes anyway.

Tavish stood so fast he nearly dumped her onto the rug. He'd already untied his boots, lost his shirt, and was in the process of unbuckling his kilt when Legend joined him in stripping without ceremony. He couldn't help but admire the man as he stood naked in their dining room, sunlight pouring in across his bronzed skin. It wasn't fair, really, that he looked like that when Tavish had to put on half a bottle of sunscreen every time he went outside with his legs exposed.

Karolena stared up at them from the beanbag, humming as she took in their display. Her gaze wandered from their sculpted chests to their erections.

"See something you want?" Tavish couldn't help but tease her.

"Would it be okay if I touched you?" She stared at the floor, her cheeks turning pink.

"Let me guess, the douche-we're-not-going-to-name-anymore wouldn't let you have your way with him?" Tavish tried not to let his disdain for the man who'd done her so wrong seep through to Karolena in any way. She was obviously as unsure of her allure as he was of his ability to gauge a beautiful woman's veracity.

"Good guess." She aimed her attention out the window again as if their "balcony" really had a soothing effect. "He only ever wanted me to lie there, still, or maybe fight to escape, but certainly never to participate. He said it made me slutty."

"He lied." Legend growled. "Probably wouldn't have been able to last more than five seconds if you had."

"About that..." Karolena groaned, before peeking up at

him again. "Is it normal? For people to do it this much, to want to do it more, and for it to take so long?"

"Who knows?" Tavish shrugged and Legend chuckled. "But that's how we do it and if you're into it, that's what we can promise you. There are advantages to having us tag team. We can take turns, and with both of us concentrating on you it feels more balanced, huh?"

Karolena blinked a few times. Then slowly, a dazzling smile stretched her lips—fuller now that they'd spent significant effort on kissing the shit out of her—and revealed bright white teeth. "Yeah, it does. Doesn't it?"

She surprised him by standing in one fluid motion, then kicking off her shoes. He desperately wanted to peel her clothes from her stitch by stitch, but when Legend took a step closer to her, he put his fingers lightly on Tavish's wrist. It was important, letting her take the reins, giving her the opportunity to decide what to reveal to them and how quickly.

Karolena started with her socks, then shoved her pants down her slender thighs. Stepping out of them, she took her ruined underwear along with them.

Tavish grinned at the reminder of their instant magnetism and how much better it was about to get. Her shirt was long enough that it covered the important stuff. "You don't have to get rid of that if you don't want to."

She fingered the hem of the black cotton as if it was a security blanket instead of a uniform. But when she took a moment to measure their intentions, she must have found them worthy.

Karolena shucked her shirt, then shrugged out of her bra, leaving her standing before them tall, lithe, angular as opposed to curvy, and so damn lovely he didn't notice at first that she was also a bit worse for wear.

"Damn, Karolena." Legend had no such problem. He crossed to her and dropped butterfly kisses over the slash of bruises that ran from her upper left shoulder to her lower right ribs. The shadow the seatbelt had left on her otherwise flawless skin was a stark reminder of where she'd come from and further proof that she'd been telling the truth.

Funny enough, Tavish hadn't doubted it. Or maybe that was par for the course, but either way it settled him to realize that much of her story had been accurate even if he despised seeing her injured.

Legend rotated her a bit so that he showed Tavish the gash on the back of her shoulder in better light than in the conference room earlier. Had they been careful enough with her before?

Tavish wasn't sure, but now that he knew what they were dealing with, he wasn't about to cause her a moment of discomfort.

"Are you sore?" he wondered aloud.

"Some." She nodded.

"I could tell you were stiff earlier. I thought it was from cleaning all day. You should have said something." Legend rubbed around the worst of the damage, gently easing her muscles.

"It would have been kind of hard to explain. Besides, I forgot about it when you were doing...stuff like that." She sighed when Legend massaged her neck, which probably had sustained whiplash.

Tavish told him, "Lay her down. Keep unwinding her."

"Where are you going?" Legend barely glanced over his shoulder as he did as he was told. Tavish didn't blame him.

"To get the first aid kit." He grabbed the container that

looked an awful lot like a tackle box from the closet. Kennedy had supplied each of them with one. With it in hand, he returned in time to see Legend rotate Karolena to her front and begin working over her back from her shoulders to her flawless ass.

It was the perfect placement for them to inspect her shoulder. "I'm no Kennedy, but let me at least cover this up so we don't open it again by accident. You should see her later for a more thorough exam."

Karolena made a vague sound of assent mixed with a moan as Legend kept tending to her too. Tavish focused on the physical damage while Legend supported her battle with emotional trauma by telling her over and over how brave and beautiful she was to open herself so fully to them.

"Still okay?" Tavish double-checked as he applied antibacterial ointment and a loose bandage to the worst of her injuries, pressing as lightly as he could while still ensuring it adhered.

"I'm sorry, are you doing something?" Karolena peeked over her shoulder at him.

Legend laughed lightly against her skin where he was kissing the upper arches of her ass while he kneaded the backs of her thighs. "Better keep up, Tav."

Tavish wouldn't lie. He'd worried early on that most women would consider him insignificant after having Legend's massive cock, but it had never been an issue. In this case, he was glad Karolena derived only pleasure from their hands. He intended to ratchet it up so she'd have no doubt he was capable of plenty.

"This is as good as I can do for now." He kissed Karolena's cheek, threw away the wrappers, then set the kit out of the way before turning his attention to erasing every bit of lassitude Legend had infused her muscles with.

Karolena shifted restlessly as Legend drove her insane with his slow seduction.

"Over there." Tavish jerked his chin toward the beanbag. "Hold her open for me."

He wasn't sure she'd be ready for a whole new level of exposure, but when Legend lifted her and sat, arranging her in his lap so her spine was cushioned by his chest and abs, she didn't wait for him to arrange her legs, splaying them over his thighs.

Instead, she stared straight into Tavish's eyes—hers brighter even than the sky behind him now—as she opened herself to him, draping her thighs over Legend's. Karolena reclined against him, her hand snaking to her mound as Legend spread his knees wider, giving Tavish room to work.

She wasn't attempting to obscure herself. Rather, she started rubbing with small circles that revealed her impatience. Tavish let her play for a moment, sure she would never have been so bold before, as Legend watched over her shoulder. His cock hung heavy between his legs, tucked partially against Karolena's ass.

The two of them together was more than Tavish could resist. He crawled to them and buried his face in Karolena's core. After breathing deep, he licked her from her clit downward until his tongue ran into Legend's dick.

"Ah, fuck." Legend groaned and his cock twitched. Tavish grabbed a handful and stroked a few times, though not too fast or too predictably. He wouldn't ruin their fun before it had begun.

Still, he toyed with Legend's dick and balls as he returned his mouth to Karolena's damp flesh. He licked sweet arousal from her opening before concentrating on her clit.

Karolena cried out his name as her fingers tangled in his hair. He was glad for its length when she fisted it and used the grip to direct him to where he pleased her most.

Legend assisted by cupping Karolena's breasts, kneading them even as his palms pressed on her nipples. When she tensed, her thighs hugging his face, Tavish paused long enough to ask. "You feel me now?"

"Uh huh." Karolena put him back where she wanted him, his mouth sucking her clit. And when he slipped two fingers inside her, reveling in the heat of her pussy smothering them, she unraveled. She bucked in Legend's hold as she pursued Tavish's lips. When his partner raked his teeth lightly along the column of her neck, Karolena damn near broke his fingers.

She turned her face toward Legend and fused her mouth to his, reveling in her newfound pastime, sharing a deep kiss with him as Tavish mimicked their motions between her legs.

After a while, Karolena squirmed and Tavish realized she was trying to get his attention. He glanced up and saw her with her arms outstretched. He went into them, rising up enough that he could take over for Legend. He kissed her too, letting her taste herself on his mouth.

Even better, she nudged his chin until he offered some to Legend, the two of them eating at each other in a frenzy inspired by her ecstasy.

"I need some of that." Legend cleaned every drop from Tavish's face before shifting.

Tavish knew exactly what his partner craved. He turned to Karolena. "More?"

"I have a lot of time to make up for." She was greedy now, not bashful, and he loved it.

Tavish hugged her, then lifted her from Legend. "Get on your back on the floor."

Legend practically dove into position. Tavish towered over him, straddling the guy, then lowered Karolena carefully so that she did too, kneeling on either side of his face. Legend wrapped his broad hands around her waist, making her appear even smaller than she was because his thumbs nearly touched near her navel.

When Legend took up where Tavish had left off, Karolena nearly tipped forward. Tavish was there, standing in front of her, his feet pointed toward Legend. That put her face at dick height.

He curled his fingers in her hair and laid one hand on her good shoulder to help her balance. But he didn't insist she do anything more than enjoy herself.

She peered up at him from beneath thick lashes. "Am I supposed to...?"

"You can do whatever you like to me, but you're not obligated to do anything at all." He rubbed her head, hopefully reminding her of Legend's gentle touches earlier. He didn't like how worrying about her next move distracted her from Legend's skilled tongue. So he stepped away to find a better angle to support her.

"No wait." Karolena reached for his hip, drawing him close. "I'd like to try. But...can you not move?"

Legend chuckled against her pussy, making her moan. Tavish would pay him back for that later.

"He's really the one with more self-control around here." Tavish pointed at Legend. "But I'll do my best."

"It's just that that son of a bitch I don't want to think about right now used to like to fuck my face. He'd choke me and laugh when I couldn't catch my breath. He wouldn't let me suck him or do anything. I had to take it."

Tavish's cock wilted a bit at that. "Mother fucker."

"Sorry." She squeezed her eyes shut until he leaned down and kissed her with long languid glides of his lips that matched whatever Legend was doing to her. After a bit, she recovered and shifted, her hand fishing for Tavish's cock.

"You have nothing to apologize for," he promised against her lips.

"I'm going to try, but I'm worried I'll freeze and not be able to finish."

Legend groaned against her and Tavish knew exactly what he was trying to say.

"He'll take care of me if you're not into it or change your mind. Besides, I'm not going to come down your throat no matter how fine your mouth is." Tavish smiled at her. "I'm saving this hard-on for your pussy."

"Not going to argue." Karolena hummed and rotated her hips, riding Legend's face.

His cock, which was thicker than ever before, told Tavish all he needed to know about how much he was enjoying eating her.

"Have at me." Tavish waved from his shoulders to his feet. He kept them planted in the carpet when she clasped his hip with one hand and ringed the base of his cock with the fingers of her other one.

It took every ounce of fortitude he possessed to stay statue still when she engulfed the head of his cock in her velvety mouth and drew on it before easing down his shaft. And when she swirled her tongue around him before pulling off again, a spurt of precome rewarded her efforts.

Karolena backed up, giving herself time to savor the taste of him and the room to breathe. When she seemed certain he wasn't going to choke her, she returned, taking him deeper and deeper until he nudged the back of her throat with the blunt tip of his shaft.

She retreated, but resumed sucking him however was comfortable for her. And it felt pretty damn fine to him.

"Hurry, Legend." Tavish didn't beg, but neither could he hold out forever.

Whatever the other guy did in response was effective. Karolena moaned around Tavish's shaft, sending vibrations straight to his balls. Her hand cupped them, rolling them around as she increased the pace of her grinding on Legend.

And right when Tavish thought he was going to have to put an end to her fun, she arched, throwing her head back so his dick left her mouth with a wet sound that he would forever associate with sex. Karolena stared at him as she shattered, coming hard on Legend.

"That's right, Karolena." Tavish held her up when she would have crashed. He cupped her face and told her, "You're so damn good at this. That felt incredible."

She lurched in his hold as wave after wave of rapture wrung her body.

"You can have whatever you desire from me." Tavish looked down at Legend, who was rolling from beneath her, as he said it.

The raised brow his partner shot him alarmed Tavish. What if it was a commitment his lovers craved instead of something physical? Or his full and complete trust, without reservations?

Somehow that didn't seem as horrifying or stupid as it had before.

12

———

Legend wiped his face with the back of his hand, then licked the glistening trail of Karolena's arousal there. He groaned, his cock pulsing with the need for direct stimulation. Even more, he craved the intimacy that came from partaking in an exchange this intense with another person—or two of them.

The only other thing that even came close in his life was being on assignment with the Shields. There was a reason the team was as tight as they were. After relying on each other in life or death circumstances, they were bonded.

After the intensity of the mutual bliss he, Tavish, and Karolena had doled out to each other that day, he knew they were becoming entwined. Potentially irrevocably.

Legend hated to push. But he had needs too. Ones that went beyond emptying his balls deep inside Karolena... though that was high on his list.

He sat up as Tavish reached down and lifted Karolena, his hand under her arms. She clung to him, wrapping her legs around him as best she could given how he'd wrecked her.

Tavish cupped her ass, holding her to him, his cock trapped between them.

"Can we get off this 'balcony' and take this to my room?" Legend surged to his feet, a bit unsteady, and approached his two lovers. He ran his fingers down Karolena's spine, smiling when she shivered and moaned.

"Are you ready to share a bed with us?" Tavish asked her as she let her head loll onto his shoulder.

"That sounds so nice right now." She practically purred. "But..."

"Yeah?" Legend was willing to meet any of her terms if it would make her comfortable while enabling him to glean some of what he needed too. Affection. Emotion. Something more than a meaningless fuck.

"I'm still not ready to be pinned down." She turned her face so it was buried against Tavish's neck.

"That's fine." Tavish kissed her forehead. "We'll be careful. And if you're ever uncomfortable, say so. Right away, okay?"

Legend fell even harder for his partner. He was doing his best. They all were, to overcome the obstacles that threatened to keep them apart indefinitely. Karolena was so much better than he'd ever been at telling Tavish what she required. Of course, he was giving it to her.

Legend realized he'd helped no one by burying his deepest desires for so long. So he took after her. "I feel close to you both. Not only skin on skin, but on another level too. I'd like to have you in my bed and I'm not sure I want you to leave."

Tavish whipped his stare to Legend. "Seriously?"

"How could you not know?"

"Even after what happened to my family because of me..."

"You've been my partner for years. You've never let me down." Legend turned and strode toward his room, hoping desperately Tavish would follow. "Don't start now. You're no coward."

"Go." Karolena hissed softly, though not quietly enough to escape Legend's hearing. "I'm good. I've always dreamed of this too, even if it's foolish and gives you both the power to hurt me, which I swore I'd never let a man do again. If I can try, so can you."

Tavish's footsteps echoed behind Legend's, making his heart sigh in relief.

His cock had never been so hard either.

They didn't waste any time celebrating. Or maybe they got straight to it. Tavish placed Karolena sideways on the bed, her ass right at the edge. He delivered one resounding spank to Legend, then handed her legs to him. "You first. I need a minute."

"Condoms," Legend reminded his friend.

"Damn, I almost forgot. We never forget."

Karolena cleared her throat. "I'm on birth control. Didn't really have an option, but right now...could we..."

"Are you saying you want us bare?" Legend clarified.

"Yeah." She bit her lip. "*He* never did that. And I guess it would make me feel like you weren't afraid of touching me. I had a physical a couple weeks ago and there's nothing else to worry about."

"Same here," Tavish told her, his cock leaking a bit at the thought. "I've never..."

"Me either." Legend looked between them both. "But I'd be lying if I said I wasn't dying to unload deep inside her, along with you."

"Ah, fuck." Tavish staggered to Legend and kissed the shit out of him, making Legend's head spin before Tavish grabbed hold of Legend's cock and guided him to Karolena. "Fuck her good, Legend. Get her ready for me because I'm not going to be able to be gentle like you once I'm buried inside her, sliding into the mess you leave behind."

Legend barely kept himself from throwing back his head and roaring. He rasped, "I have a better idea."

"What could be better than that?" Karolena wondered, sounding as dazed as she looked as she stared up at them from his bed. "Unless it's both of you."

Tavish smiled. "Yeah, we'll come inside her together. I'm going to shoot all over your cock while her pussy wrings our dicks."

Karolena's eyes went wide. "Is that actually possible?"

"Only if it doesn't cause you any pain." Tavish climbed onto the bed and knelt near her uninjured shoulder. This time she didn't hesitate. She turned her head and licked his shaft, making Legend the teensiest bit jealous. "Let him open you up before we try it, okay?"

She nodded, dragging her mouth along Tavish's erection. He groaned.

Legend couldn't stand being outside her a moment longer. He fisted his cock and tapped it on her clit a few times, loving the damp smack his heavy flesh made on hers. She sighed and arched toward him, her body as greedy as his for more of the pleasure they seemed able to bring each other so effortlessly.

Tavish reached between her legs and spread her pussy for Legend, so he fit the head of his cock to her opening and began to push. She accepted him much more easily than she had earlier, the remnants of her orgasms easing his way through the rings of her muscles.

Karolena's toes curled where her feet were propped on the edge of the bed, her knees bent sharply. As soon as Legend had fit himself into her fully, he hooked his hands beneath her knees and lifted them. His balls pressed against her as he rocked, making her call out his name— though clearly with passion and not pain.

"Go ahead," Tavish directed him, ensuring she was okay. She could handle them.

As Legend began to move, lightning flashed through each nerve-ending in his dick and spread outward, illuminating and electrifying every bit of him. He grunted and dug in, meeting each upward flex of Karolena's hips with a thrust of his own. Knowing neither of them had a chance at lasting, Tavish ran his hand down Karolena's center until he could strum her clit.

She instantly clamped on Legend, risking tipping him into orgasm long before he was ready.

There was no way in hell he was going to spill inside her before they at least tried to have Tavish join him, being held together by her body. It was the stuff of his fantasies. The most illicit ones he'd ever had. Ones he'd always been too scared to speak out loud because he'd known Tavish hadn't been ready to hear them.

Was he now?

Legend looked to his best friend. The other man was splitting his attention, watching Karolena toying with his own cock and making sure she was okay, then stealing glimpses of Legend and how well he was fucking her. There was no way Legend was going to make it long enough to help her over the edge one more time so she was relaxed when they double-teamed her.

"Tavish, help." He pulled out, choking the base of his dick with tight fingers.

"I've got you. Both of you," Tavish cooed when Karolena whimpered at the loss.

He helped her rise onto all fours on Legend's bed, this time with her head facing the pillows. "How's your shoulder?"

"Fine." She shocked them both by biting Tavish's thigh. "Or it will be if someone fucks me. Right now."

Tavish's laughter was wicked. In the best sense. He clambered behind her and slid home in a single deep stroke that had him completely sheathed in Karolena. She pounded the mattress with her fists, then shouted, "Yes! Move, damn it."

Legend had intended to give himself more time to recover, but when he heard her desperation, it mirrored his. He couldn't help but climb onto the head of the bed and offer his dick to her. She licked him, tentatively testing her ability to take him. And though she couldn't swallow much, she sucked on the tip while Tavish rode her furiously from behind. His face grew red as he stared at the ceiling as if praying for stamina.

But he didn't need to, because just then, Karolena went stiff between them and began to jerk in time to the spasms rippling through her. Before she'd finished coming, Tavish had rolled them to their sides, still buried inside her as he extended her climax with occasional pumps.

Legend knew it was time. To see if this would work. If she was ready. If any of them were.

"You still want to try this? To take us both? To have us fill you up so you have no doubts about how badly we want you?" Tavish's string of dirty talk got to both Karolena and Legend.

She opened her eyes and crooked her finger at Legend.

He went, stretching out in front of her even as Tavish spooned her from behind, still ensconced in her body.

"Is this okay?" he checked.

She nodded.

"You don't feel trapped?" He couldn't risk a misstep. Not now, when he could tell that she was so different from every other woman they'd shared before. She could be theirs. The missing piece they'd been searching for.

"No. I'm good. So good." She put her arm around him and tried to tug him closer, though of course he was far too large to budge.

But neither did he intend to deny her. So he cozied up to her front as Tavish raised her top leg for him. Legend took his cock in hand once again. This time he traced the base of Tavish's cock and slid up it until he prodded her opening, already stretched to permit Tavish inside.

It took some doing, but he began to make progress, fitting himself into her beside his best friend and partner. "Fuck. Yes."

Tavish did his job. He made sure they weren't doing anything she didn't crave. "Karolena? How is it?"

She moaned. Words lost, intentions plain. She grabbed Legend's flank and tugged him toward her, feeding herself more of his cock. He rubbed along the length of Tavish's erection inside her warm, wet grasp.

Karolena's body cocooned them together, increasing the friction as they glided along each other's shafts. Maybe it was the lack of condoms, but Legend thought it was something else that rocketed their shared experience easily into the slot of best sex of his life.

When he caught Tavish's knowing stare, he leaned forward and sealed his mouth to the other guy's. He fucked Karolena as he made out with Tavish. Their passionate exchange only served to spiral Karolena higher. She began to moan with every forward motion of his hips, so he concentrated on making sure to rub the root of his dick across her clit on every pass.

It was so good, he did it over and over, faster and faster, trying to absorb as much of the ecstasy he was generating for the three of them. Nothing that incredible could last forever.

"I'm going to—" Karolena tried to warn them, but it wasn't necessary. The rhythmic clenches of her body told them everything they needed to know moments before she succumbed to her most powerful orgasm yet.

There was no way either he or Tavish could prevent themselves from joining her.

Tavish called to him, "Now, Legend! Let go now."

As if he could have held back. The first hot pulse of Tavish's release on Legend's dick triggered his own explosion. He shot jet after jet of come as deep into Karolena as he could manage, flooding her pussy as Tavish did the same. They plunged into the slippery mixture they deposited within her as an endless rush of rapture drained them.

And when the most passionate parts of the storm of pleasure ebbed, neither he nor Tavish budged. Karolena hummed between them, her eyes fluttering open as a slow, wide smile decorated her face. "I had no idea it could be like that."

"Me either," Tavish echoed.

The thing was...Legend had thought all along that it was a possibility. He just never expected that they would find the person to unlock this level of unity between them. Because Tavish hadn't been ready. And now that he might be, Legend wasn't sure that he was going to survive.

Worse yet, he was terrified that if they didn't resolve Karolena's issues with Vladimir, they could lose her after barely discovering all his fantasies could actually become reality.

The stakes suddenly got so much higher.

Legend wrapped his arms around both Karolena and Tavish, thrilled when neither of them balked. Exhausted, and thoroughly satisfied, they drifted into sleep, trusting him to protect them. He swore then and there, to himself and to them—even if they didn't know it—that he would never let them down and never let them go.

13

―――――

Karolena had officially lost track of time. It had definitely been more than a couple days since her entire universe had shifted. Less than a week, she was pretty sure. It was hard to tally given her initial shock, jet lag, the stress of trying to blend into a strange land, her rush to find work, and then the utter relaxation that had followed once the Shields had convinced her she'd landed in a safe haven.

She'd slept hard those first few nights after she'd confessed who she really was and Legend and Tavish had claimed her as both their assignment and their pleasure. Since then, she'd spent her days exploring an entirely different world full of possibilities. Plus sitting for interviews to divulge everything she could about Vladimir's operations. And cleaning. *Blech.*

It was the only part of her experience at Shields she didn't enjoy. The good stuff, like Legend and Tavish taking her to new heights every night—and a few times during each day, too—and actually having people around that she was coming to think of as friends far outweighed her annoyance with the number of times she'd wiped fingerprints from the stainless fridge in the communal kitchen.

So when James announced to everyone gathered in the common area that he had something to show them outside, Karolena set her trusty mop down and wandered out to the parking lot behind Shields headquarters along with Laurel and Aven, probably the pair she'd spent the most time getting to know aside from Legend and Tavish. It was nice to have someone who understood how difficult it was to transition to a new normal, though she hated that Laurel—and one of her boyfriends, Jace—could relate to her trafficking trauma. Aven was a great listener and seemed eager to hang out, having only recently moved into Shields headquarters herself. She seemed a bit lonely, though Karolena figured that made sense since Aven was the only single resident at the moment. Karolena was happy to keep her company and hopefully return a tiny bit of the kindness they'd shown her.

The guys followed right behind them, shooting the shit with Laurel's other boyfriend, Nolan, plus Ace and Liam. Despite how casual they seemed, Karolena noticed Legend subconsciously pat his holster, where he wore one of his guns at his hip. She was sure every other agent was doing the same since a couple of days ago Devra and Morgan had successfully delivered their message to the men who'd been looking for her.

Karolena blinked against the harsh glare of the sun like a bear emerging from its cave after hibernation.

"You've been cooped up a while now." Aven handed her a pair of aviator sunglasses. "Here, take these."

"Ah, thanks." Karolena sighed when they diminished the impact of the laser-like rays.

"How are you handling that?" Laurel asked quietly. "It bothers me, even now, when I'm unable to leave somewhere."

"Fortunately, Legend and Tavish have been distracting me, but...this does feel awfully nice." Karolena breathed deep, inhaling the crisp scent of the greenery she had spied from the windows above and the tracts of pine trees she knew weren't too far away.

Aven hummed. "It does. Don't forget you can set up therapy and Jordan will cover it. Kennedy has the info."

"I already started a couple days ago." Karolena wasn't going to pretend like she didn't need help adjusting. "It's going to take a while to work through everything, but it's helping to have someone impartial to talk to about all the transitions I'm going through."

"Don't forget we're always here for you too." Laurel gave her a quick hug. "It does get easier to believe this is real and that no one's going to take it away from you after a while."

Of course she'd nailed it. Karolena had woken up in a cold sweat most mornings, afraid it had all been a spectacular dream and she was still a prisoner in her previous miserable existence.

Aven agreed. "There's a reason I fly things. I like to be self-sufficient more than I should. Probably because I could never count on anyone until I met these folks."

Before Karolena or Laurel could ask any follow up questions to her revelation, they were joined by more and more people. It shocked Karolena how sprawling their network of friends was; the Shields had to know at least half of Middletown.

"Hey, Blakely!" Aven waved to one of the newcomers, then introduced the other woman to Karolena. "This is

Legend and Tavish's girlfriend, Karolena. Karolena, Blakely is our resident tattoo artist. I didn't realize you would be here today. Who's getting new art?'

Trying to keep up with the conversation while jotting a note in her mental contact book about Blakely—remnants of her faux-socialite past—Karolena didn't have a chance to process the *girlfriend* label right away. Was that what she was?

She glanced over her shoulder at Tavish, who shot her an encouraging smile, but she wasn't sure if he'd heard Aven's declaration or if he was simply kind and supportive in general.

"No one." Blaklely beamed. "Dave told me the permit finally came through for my parlor, even though neither of us was able to reach my dad to find out what the holdup on the permits was or how it finally got resolved. He's been handling all that stuff so he must have squared it away, though it's weird he didn't let me know. Anyway, they're going to break ground this afternoon. Finally!"

Karolena ran through her previous knowledge. Dave. He was one of the Powertools. The construction workers James and his spouses had a polyamorous relationship with. If she remembered right, he was the big guy—who kind of reminded her of Legend, in a gentle giant sort of way.

Blakely pointed at the cement truck pulling into the lot then. It parked in the far corner where it was easy to maneuver without risking clipping another vehicle and out of the way. Its drum rotated slowly as Dave got out from behind the wheel and ambled over to them with a limp he couldn't quite hide. He was accompanied by a tall, handsome man named Joe, whom she'd met before. He was married to Morgan from the bakery on the corner, so he stopped by often after visiting her.

"That's fantastic. Congratulations." Laurel turned to Aven and Karolena. "We should go over to the construction site after this for moral support since her dad isn't going to be there."

"Thanks for inviting me. I would love to, but I'm probably not allowed." Karolena tried not to pout. "I'm surprised these two even let me out long enough for this."

Of course she'd heard the full details of Ruby's prior kidnapping by then, but everyone was on full alert and they weren't about to let her straggle. Surrounded by this many Shields, she was well-protected.

"Okay, James, what are we here for?" Jordan asked from where he stood nearby, hugging Wren from behind.

James beamed, practically bouncing in his neon pink, high-top canvas sneakers, skinny jeans, and sky-blue tank top with white edging. Before he could explain, the roar of engines blasted through the streets, waking up the sleepy town, bouncing off the brick facades of the stores that lined the main street. A flash of green caught Karolena's attention just before a tiny, ridiculous vehicle zipped into the lot and screeched to a stop a bit away from the crowd, near where Dave had left his truck.

The rest of the entourage, including a gleaming purple muscle car and a man riding a navy blue motorcycle parked before yet more people joined their growing audience.

The bright green car with flames painted over the hood and down the sides was hard to look away from. A tall black pipe stuck out from the far side of its front. Its wheels were enormous for how compact it was. Dark windows obscured the interior. A man climbed from it and jogged toward them before tossing the keys to James.

He hugged them to his chest and sighed, "My baby. You're home."

Karolena looked to Legend, who was cracking up too hard to fill her. So Aven did it for him, shaking her head. "James's car has been though some shit. Every time it gets beat up, he's had our friends at Hot Rods fix it and make it even tougher. Those two, from the purple car, are Roman and his husband, Carver. And the guy on the motorcycle is Quinn, Roman's little brother."

"He owns the motorcycle shop where Wren does her welding, right?" Karolena thought she was starting to get the full picture.

"Not exactly. Gavyn owns it. Quinn's the manager there." Laurel waved to the guy. "That's where I stayed when I first came to town. He's married to Devra from Sweet & Spicy and their husband, Trevon."

Karolena observed the mechanics, who circled around James while talking animatedly about the latest enhancements to his vehicle. "Remind me who the guy driving James's car is?"

Aven filled her in. "That's Holden. He's the Hot Rod's interior upholstery specialist. His wife, Sabra, is the one who produces their reality TV show. Plus they do this super cool couples acro-yoga shit together. You should ask to see it sometime. I'm sure it comes in handy to be that flexible when you sometimes hook up with like eleven people at once."

Karolena was grateful for the sunglasses then so they couldn't see her eyes bugging out. *Damn.* And here she thought she was greedy for keeping Legend and Tavish all to herself. They were plenty for her to attempt to handle.

The visitors mingled with the Shields. Whether on purpose or by instinct each cluster of agents staked themselves out on the perimeter of the gathering. Kennedy, Knox, and Marcus chatted with the Hot Rods on one corner while Sola, Aarav, and Cash caught up with Quinn on the opposite side of James. Ruby, Liam, and Ace stood up front while Legend and Tavish shadowed Karolena near the rear of the assembly, behind a sea of friends. Jordan, Wren, and Kason were at the heart of it all.

James spoke up then so everyone could hear him. "To shut up those of you who make fun of my baby once and for all, we've prepared a demonstration to show you that everything we survive makes us stronger."

Karolena couldn't help but shake her head at their tomfoolery. She'd never had a sibling, but she imagined this was what it would be like if you got along with them well...and had thirty of them.

"Who's *we*?" Jordan asked, a long-suffering grimace on his face.

James pointed across the street to where the massive garage doors of Middletown's fire station began to rise. Foot by foot, they revealed the florescent boots of four firefighters then their black turnout gear, edged in more yellow. Several of the women, and some of the guys, cheered and whistled for the group that she'd seen featured in a sexy firefighter calendar on the breakroom wall.

"What are they carrying?" she wondered out loud.

"Is that a flamethrower?" Liam asked.

"That is *so* cool." Ace practically drooled. "Do you think they'll let me have a turn?"

Jordan cut him off right there. "Absolutely not."

"You just got the car back again, babe. Are you sure you want to do this?" James's wife, Devon, held his hand. "I know how much you love it. Almost more than me."

"Don't be ridiculous." James rolled his eyes as if it was his wife who was over the top and kissed her right there in front of everyone. Karolena wasn't used to such public and affectionate displays, but it made her heart flip-flop. "The only thing I love almost as much as you is Neil."

"Hey." Neil's laughter took the sting out of his indignation.

"Besides, it's fine," Roman promised. "We used a coating that deflects heat and also reinforced all the surfaces with blast-resistant technology usually reserved for things like the Popemobile. He's all good. We're going to take some video clips so Sabra can add them to our commercials for street racing clients."

By the time Devon had been reassured, the firefighters had jogged over, carrying the giant silver tube and a couple of super-sized extinguishers. She hoped the safety equipment was an unnecessary precaution. A woman drove over a firetruck with the lights on but no sirens and parked it so that it blocked the entrance to the lot and was accessible in case of emergency.

"Hey, Jordan." The man with the most patches on his jacket saluted the head of Shields.

"Bored, Karis?" A corner of Jordan's mouth twitched as he ribbed the chief.

"The boys needed a few more training exercise credits." Karis grinned back. "Plus, who doesn't want to play with a flamethrower?"

"Me." Karolena was both amused and apprehensive given their antics. She took a step back and bumped into Legend's broad chest. It shocked her how she instantly settled against him, less anxious. Even more so when Tavish angled himself so that she was exposed as little as possible. Their arms instinctively went around her.

Quinn took notice, smiling when he realized exactly how familiar her guards were with her body. She braced herself but all he said, quietly, was "Congratulations."

She didn't know exactly how to answer, though she caught Tavish fist-bump the man. The firefighters lining up in front of James's car and the whole crowd counting down saved her from formulating a response.

Three...two...

If they shouted *one*, she didn't hear it over the whoosh of the inferno that shot from the fire gun directly at James's poor, precious car. They paused after the first blast to assess the vehicle. Miraculously, it seemed fine, like the Hot Rods had promised.

So they cranked it up and did it again. The flames were twice as big this time and so hot they glowed blue at the core. Karolena figured that's what she would look like if anyone took an infrared picture of her while Tavish and Legend were setting her off.

The guys around them whooped and cheered as James's car withstood the onslaught of feverish blast that she could feel all the way from where she was standing. She fanned her face as her upper lip and the dips below her eyes grew damp with a sheen of perspiration.

Which was when she heard it.

A piercing alarm was followed by an amber light flashing on the rear of Dave's cement mixer, just beyond James's car. Though it was safely out of the line of fire, the heat must have pissed it off somehow.

Immediately, the firefighters cut the fuel and whipped their attention to Karis for direction. Karolena could tell they were a unit as well-trained and cohesive as the Shields. They operated as one as they assessed the issue.

Karis looked to Dave. "What's it doing?"

"Uh oh." Dave's eyes grew wide.

James, also having spent decades in the construction business with his friends, cursed. "No. No! We have to move the car."

"You can't touch the door handle," Roman cautioned. "Or any part of the vehicle. It'll melt your hand off."

Joe, the other Powertools foreman, grabbed James's elbow and prevented him from sprinting toward his baby as Devon and Neil tried to calm him down. At the same time, the drum of the cement mixer began to tip.

"It's a safety feature." Dave groaned. "If it senses too high of a temperature in the mix, it assumes the cement is kicking off and dumps it to prevent it from hardening inside the truck and ruining it."

"Oh, it's going to ruin something all right." Ace seemed to blurt what they were all thinking but knew better than to say most times. This was no exception. He added, "Wow. It goes a lot faster than I would have thought."

The drum had inclined enough that the first thick plops of the cement poured from the truck onto the roof of James's car. Rocks and slurry quickly obscured the colorful paintjob with gray sludge that sizzled as it ran down the sides like grotesque icing.

"We have heat-proof gloves." One of the firefighters was already tugging them on past his elbows.

"No. Don't." Holden shook his head.

"What do you mean *no*?" James rounded on Holden as he dangled the keys out toward the firefighter.

"If you open the door, it'll ruin the entire interior and

my leatherwork. You ordered it jizz proof, not cement proof!" Holden threw his hands in the air as half the people around them laughed and half stared in horror.

"How the hell do you fuck in something that small?" Ace clearly still had his mind on the important questions.

"Let the cement inside and we'll never get it all out," Holden insisted.

An entire waterfall of viscous mud began dumping on top of the car. It was too late to stop it. So they watched as the pile of cement with the car at its center grew larger and larger.

"Don't worry, the car is waterproof." Dave tried to downplay the situation. "The Heat can use their hoses and wash this right off. No problem."

Karolena had seen that nickname on the calendar too. The Heat. Must have been easier than saying Middletown City Fire Department all the time. Catchier, too.

"Wow. That thing really holds a lot of cement, huh?" Tavish winced.

As the weight on top of the car increased, an ominous metallic creak cut through the sound of the plopping cement and the bang of rocks pummeling the roof. Suddenly the entire mound shuddered and dropped a bit lower.

"Uh oh." Dave said again.

Carver stopped recording his video. She figured this wouldn't make good advertisement after all. Instead, he started texting furiously. "I'm letting Eli know we're going to need a new suspension. A much more robust one."

More sounds, this time with more of a crumpling component.

More texting. "And maybe some impact reinforcement for crush resistance."

James pasted a smile on his face that had nothing in common with his usual ones. "This is fine. Everything's fine."

The pile quickly turned into something that resembled a gray version of the poop emoji but without eyes or a smile and with the addition of a random black snorkel poking out the top of it.

After a few more slow revolutions, the cement truck unleashed the last of its load onto James's car, then emitted a cheery triple-beep before tucking the drum neatly back into place and going silent.

"On the bright side, maybe my dad will be able to make the groundbreaking after all since we'll need to reschedule." Blakely had clearly gone to the same school of positive reframing that James had.

"I'm sorry, Blakely." James turned around and offered her a hug, which she gladly accepted.

"Someday this will be funny," she promised him.

"Oh, it's fucking hilarious right now." Ace snorted, though Liam smacked him in the gut with the back of his hand, having no impact whatsoever on his rock-hard abs or his inability to keep his thoughts private.

The Heat didn't waste any time. As soon as the cement truck finished doing its thing, they navigated around the oozing heap and hooked their hoses to the nearest hydrant. Efficient and serious, they began spraying down the mess and dispersing it so that it wouldn't harden into an even worse problem. With the force of their professional equipment, it didn't take long before they uncovered enough of James's car to see it had been squished.

Neil pinched the bridge of his nose. "Can you just let Devon or me drive you places in our trucks? Please?"

James craned his neck to evaluate the damage. "Why? I'm short. There's probably still plenty of headroom. It's fine."

Devon muttered under her breath about stubborn men but shot her husbands a rueful smile nonetheless.

"We'll fix this," Holden promised. "I don't know how, but we'll figure it out together like we always do. And when we bring your baby back next time, it will be smash-proof too. Okay?"

He clapped James on the shoulder.

But whatever James said or was about to was drowned out by a ringing in Karolena's ears. She went ramrod straight as her instincts encouraged her to flee.

"Karolena?" Legend spread his legs and put his hand on his weapon. "What's wrong?"

Tavish did the same, following her line of sight down the street toward Sweet & Spicy, where her vision tunneled in on an approaching figure. Even at a distance, she knew exactly who it was.

"Levin," she whispered.

"Him?" Aven gawked. "Damn. Why are the bad boys always the hottest?"

Was he coming as her friend or as one of Vladimir's minions, no matter how powerful he was in his own right?

"Get down." Jordan covered his pregnant wife until he dragged their husband on top of her, then shot back to his feet, his weapon drawn and aimed in Levin's direction.

The rest of the Shields did the same. Within moments, Levin found himself staring down more than a dozen barrels.

"Holy shit." Quinn, like all the Hot Rods and Powertools and even the Heat, crouched as Jordan had commanded to stay out of their way. "I'm glad I'm just a mechanic."

Levin, however, didn't so much as flinch. He kept walking, no faster and no slower. He held his hands up, palms facing them, seemingly unfazed as he closed the distance between them. He was and always had been a badass. When he was within earshot, he said, "I only came because you insisted and this is the welcome I get?"

"You'll understand we're the cautious sort," Jordan responded. "Don't come any closer until we give you permission. And if you drop your hand so much as an inch, we will shoot you."

"Karolena, what the hell is going on?" Levin did as instructed but otherwise ignored Jordan. He looked from her and her veritable army of protectors to the gigantic mess surrounding James's car. "This is exactly the kind of shit I was trying to keep you away from. Well, plus whatever that is."

Jordan shook his head. "This isn't the place to discuss it."

"Where do you want him, boss?" Legend asked, his chest rumbling against Karolena's back. Levin's eyes narrowed as he took in Legend and Tavish's possessive stance.

"No one came with you?" Jordan verified. "Not even in town somewhere."

"Only me. Your instructions weren't difficult to understand." Levin still didn't look away from Karolena, as if asking silently if she was okay.

She smiled, hoping to give him some reassurance and deescalate the situation. But even having him there, in the midst of her newfound serenity, made her uneasy.

"Everyone who doesn't work here is going—right now,

not one single excuse—to Hot Rods until I tell them they can come back. Except for the Heat. They're returning to their station. If we don't call them every fifteen minutes and tell them otherwise, they're going to open the black lockbox I put in Karis's lower left desk drawer." He stared at the chief, who nodded. "It has directions and contact information for people who will know what to do. Under no circumstances is anyone to enter this building until I give the all clear."

It reassured Karolena that he had a plan, but also offended her that they were treating Levin like the enemy. She edged toward him, but Legend stopped her, looping his arm around her waist. When she tested his hold, he didn't budge, pissing her off. "He's not going to hurt anyone."

"We don't take chances with our loved ones," Jordan said, not unkindly.

James smiled at her. "That includes you."

"Nolan, Marcus, please escort our guest into the holding room and make sure he's not bringing anything in with him," Jordan ordered.

Levin glared when the men each snagged one of his arms and forced him toward the entry. They weren't gentle. Nor was it in his nature to be submissive.

"Don't be so rough with him. Please." Karolena reached toward Levin. "He's my—"

"Lover?" Tavish hissed. "I knew it."

Levin whipped his head around at that, staring at Tavish as if he'd declared he really enjoyed getting punched in the nuts or something equally absurd.

"Friend." She glared at Tavish. "I trusted you, but I guess you were never going to be able to do the same. Were you?"

Why did that hurt so much? She'd barely known him a week but somehow, she'd thought she'd already started living her future rather than having a fling to pass the time until forever came along.

Laurel gave Karolena a quick hug and whispered in her ear, "He didn't mean that. He's worried about losing you. Stay safe and we'll talk later." Then she accepted Jace's outstretched hand and headed off with him in the direction of Sweet & Spicy with the rest of the non-Shields.

"What about my car? Is it going to get stuck in the rest of that cement and become a monument at Shields forever?" James pouted as he abandoned the wreckage so he could join Jordan at the head of the pack. After them came Karolena, who was surrounded by a living wall of assassins intent on keeping her alive instead of killing her.

Too bad one of them had already stabbed her in the heart.

14

—————

Karolena released her held breath in a long, shaky exhale when Nolan and Marcus escorted Levin into the boardroom. They pushed him into a spot directly across the table from her where she was wedged between Legend and Tavish. Except, unlike before, she didn't take any solace in being flanked by them.

How could she when they obviously didn't have any faith in her despite coaxing her into depending on them?

Marcus said, "He's clean. No weapons and no communications."

"Good." Jordan leaned back as if he was completely at ease with their meeting.

Well, that made one of them. Karolena's tension was rooting mostly in anger and bitterness. Embarrassment also now that Levin kept flicking his too-astute gaze between her, Legend, and Tavish. Sure, he'd known some of her darkest secrets, about how horribly Vladimir had treated her, but she'd been forced into that relationship.

What would he think if he knew what she had chosen to do with her independence, and so soon after he'd helped her break free?

After Tavish's outburst, he'd probably think she was an idiot. And maybe she was.

Karolena shoved on the arms of their chairs, then said under her breath, without looking at either of them, "Can you give me some space here?"

Levin frowned and so did Jordan. She had to remember they were spies and damn good ones. Men who could read a hell of a lot into the barest twitches of her expression.

Tavish scooted his chair a few inches away and huffed. Did he get that he'd put the distance between them when he'd questioned her commitment?

"Stop digging your hole deeper, bro," Ace muttered from Tavish's other side. "Even I can see you're not doing yourself any favors."

"I've come a long way to sit here while you bicker." Levin sneered at them.

From beside him, Aven fanned her cheeks with her hand. Was it because of the weather, the failed demonstration, or because of Levin's fieriness?

After a lingering look at her, Levin shifted his attention to Jordan. "Who are you and why did you want me to come?"

"My name is Jordan Mikalski. Officially, I'm a retired government agent who runs a security services firm in the middle of nowhere."

"You can say that again." Levin glanced out the window at the pond behind the parking lot. Middletown was a far cry from Saint Petersburg. One of the reasons

Karolena had already fallen in love with the place, even if it didn't have the more sophisticated comforts of the metropolis she'd enjoyed back home. "And off the record?"

"We handle problems my old office never could considering the bureaucracy and politics involved. We don't leave paper trails and we don't ask permission. When someone reaches out to us, it's always about a matter that has broad implications for society but is...messy."

"Got it. You're assassins with morals. That's cute." Levin crossed his arms and shook his head. He caught on a lot faster than she had. He flicked his stare to Karolena. "How the hell did you get mixed up with this gang when you'd barely escaped ours?"

"Pure, dumb luck." Her shoulders slumped. At first she'd thought it had been fortuitous, now she wasn't convinced.

Neither was Levin. "I'm not sure that's what I'd call it."

"It is." Jordan laid his palms flat on the table, along with his cards. "Taking down her ex is the only way Karolena will never have to look over her shoulder again. We can make that happen."

"What do you think, *sestra*? Are they helping you by going after our pal Vlad or did they somehow draw you to them because they had it out for him anyway and you are a convenient tool?" Levin hadn't risen to his position simply because his father had held it before him. He was a match for the Shields in every way.

"I believed it was the former." Karolena rubbed her temples. Had they been playing mind games to get her to cooperate? To lure Levin there?

"I'm not trying to second guess you, but you don't have much experience with the way things really work. And even simple kindnesses probably seem like grand gestures to you." Levin sighed. "Have you told them what a prick your husband is?"

"He doesn't deserve that title in my eyes," James cut in. "Not if he bought her and kept her when she was too young and powerless to object."

"Oh, that was nothing compared to the rest." Levin drew a deep breath, then looked at her with so much pity she was sure she was going to hate whatever came out of his mouth next. "How do you think her mom got 'sick' in the first place? And how do you think Vladimir knew about it? He saw her at the ballet one night, getting a refreshment for her daughter during intermission."

No, no, no.

Karolena remembered that night vividly. Her mother had gone for a snack and never returned. It was only when she heard commotion in the lobby that she'd gone out and discovered her mom had lost consciousness in the bathroom, never to wake up again. But she hadn't known anything about Vladimir then. Only weeks after had he shown up at her hospital bed with a very generous offer...

She whimpered.

"I'm sorry, *sestra*. I wasn't even eighteen yet myself."

Aven turned more fully toward Levin, her eyes gleaming with mercy and anger on behalf of the boy he'd been.

"I didn't understand the extremes Vladimir would go to and certainly didn't know what he intended when he followed your mother into the restroom and tried to get her to go home with him. When she refused, he didn't take it well. You know how he is."

She did.

"She fought him, and in the struggle she slipped and hit her head on the sink on the way down." Levin cursed in Russian under his breath. "Vladimir was quick to pay off the staff to keep them from remembering they saw him coming out of the bathroom before he told them they needed to call the paramedics."

Karolena tried to breathe through the bands constricting her chest. It sounded exactly like something he would do. Levin met her gaze, lending credence to his account.

Legend turned to her with soothing words she couldn't understand through her agony. So much made sense in an instant.

"He was cruel to you, I know. For years," Levin told her. "But even more so because it was never you he really wanted. It's just that you look so much like her and she made him so angry. He can't stand not getting what he wants. Every time he saw you, it was a reminder."

Relief warred with disgust and fury inside her. This explained everything.

"I'm not trying to make excuses for my part, standing by and not objecting—even if that would have gotten me in a similar situation—but it took me a long time to realize that the way I was raised isn't the way I want to be anymore. And once I came to that conclusion, I had to make things right with you. That's why I was willing to take the risk to get you out of there. You never deserved any of it, and neither did your mother. I'm so sorry."

Legend growled. "I wanted to kill him before. Now I want to make him suffer."

"It's not that easy." Levin scrubbed his hands over his eyes as if he was tired, something she'd never seen from him before. It wasn't a good idea to show weakness in front of Vladimir. Could Levin tell the Shields were different too? "Vladimir assumes I'm bringing her back with me. I convinced him a rival organization shipped her over here and that I'd take care of them. What the hell am I going to tell him now? He's ruthless, but he's not stupid."

Jordan shakes his head. "You don't have to tell him anything. That's not how this is going to go."

A pregnant pause filled the room. Even Karolena understood what Jordan was implying. An excuse wasn't necessary if Vladimir wasn't around long enough to need duping.

"Fine, I'll get rid of him for you, no problem. I fucking hate that bastard for my own reasons." Levin acted like it was nothing to take someone's life. How many times had he done it before and what could Vladimir have possibly done to cross a line with someone who had grown up in a world that violent and cold? "There have been rumblings about shaking up the management for a while. Vladimir hasn't made a lot of friends, you know? But you should be aware I don't intend to leave the country or even the organization, for that matter. So we're going to have to do this in a way that covers my ass."

Karolena knew him well enough to tell that there was something he wasn't saying. Something he cared about besides the mafia. He didn't have any more say in his role there than she had. And she'd bet he'd abandon his post in a heartbeat, if he could.

She sat extra still, afraid to tip off any of the Shields about what she was picking up on. After all, Levin had been honest with her, and Tavish...not so much. He still didn't fully believe her and maybe never would.

"I have a much better idea." Jordan had clearly already thought of his approach. "We've heard Vlad's too careful for our sniper Aarav to pick him off easily."

"Yeah, he's been head of this organization a long time. Not by chance." Levin sighed as if he'd already considered all of the possibilities and dismissed them.

Jordan nodded as the rest of the Shields paid close attention to the plan. "So find a way to let Legend and Tavish and their guns in. Tell Vladimir they have Karolena and want to negotiate. Or tell him nothing but somehow take them home with you. They will eliminate him for you. As head of security, you put your worst guys on a particular exit, let my agents know which one, and they'll handle the rest."

Levin spoke slowly then as if Jordan was a lot dumber than he'd originally thought. "Killing Vlad isn't going to do shit to stop the organization. Someone else will take his place."

Jordan, deadpan, said, "I know."

Then he simply stared at Levin.

"Me? No. No way." Levin swiped his hands in front of him as if shoving the idea itself away. "I've been turning down the job from the inside for years. I don't want to get any deeper than I already am."

"Even better." Jordan sat back then. "It's a temporary assignment. Let us put you in place and work on how to unravel the whole thing. Permanently."

"Damn," Legend whispered as if even he was a bit impressed with Jordan's balls.

"No," Levin refused again. "It's too risky. And there are...other...considerations."

There it was again. Karolena sat up straighter and

wondered who it was he was trying to protect in addition to her. He cut his stare to her, then back to Jordan.

"We're not exactly asking." The head of Shields was scarier than she'd realized. Had Levin been right? Had the agents preyed on her weakness to hospitality? Had they used positive manipulation to bend her to their will instead of Vladimir's cruel approach?

She needed some time alone. To think about how her world was mutating again and to ground herself so she could figure out what was right and what was real.

"Congratulations on your promotion," James added in his patented chipper style.

Levin stood, putting the Shields on edge. But all he did was pace. In that moment, Karolena realized he'd been every bit as trapped as she had.

She rose too and went to him, fuck whatever Tavish and Legend thought. She took his forearms in her hands and held tight. He looked straight into her eyes and said again, "I'm sorry."

"I forgive you for anything you might have done." She threw caution out the window and went in for a full hug. She needed it and she suspected he did too.

When he didn't pull away, and instead held her for a moment before sighing, she looked over her shoulder at Jordan. "Can I speak to Levin in private for a few minutes? Or even switch to Russian if you don't want to let him out of your sights?"

Jordan grimaced. "No, I can't let you do that."

"So that stuff you told me about how I could be one of you, and how you loved me..." She looked directly at James for that one. He shifted his stare to his sneakers. "It was all bullshit? Not one damn one of you trusts me after I put my faith in you?"

Aven spoke up then. "That's not it, Karolena. We don't trust that sexy son of a bitch not to use you."

Damn it. Frankly, she hated it, but she could see their point. She returned her focus to Levin. "Fine. Tell me then. Why do you want to stay? And what caused you to change these past couple of years? I've felt it. And I can see it today...there's a reason. What is it?'

Levin swallowed hard. "I'll tell you if you explain why that redhead in the kilt and his giant sidekick were so pissed when they thought we might have a thing. Are they using you? Have they forced you to do...stuff...with them in exchange for their help? Because if so, this is off. No deal."

"No. Sleeping with them was my prerogative, though maybe not the wisest decision I've made considering how they've acted this afternoon." She shrugged. "Either way, I liked it and they're good at it, when they're not practicing on each other."

Levin blinked several times in rapid succession as if he wasn't sure he'd heard her correctly.

So James clarified. "We like to share around here. At least within limits. These amateurs keep themselves to their trios. My husband and my wife and I have an arrangement with six of our friends. As you do."

"Your husband?" Levin latched onto that.

Karolena braced herself, considering how hateful Vladimir had been when discussing homosexuality.

"I'm not trying to pry." Levin looked back to her as if it pained him to ask for details. "But are you saying that the three of you are in some kind of relationship where the two guys also..."

"Yes, that's exactly what she's saying," Legend boomed, daring Levin to say one dumb thing. If anything, she didn't doubt his love for Tavish. Because it was obvious that's what it was. She'd seen it up close and personal.

"Huh." Tension melted from Levin's body. She wondered if she'd ever seen him at anything other than full alert before. "Okay, then I will do what you ask."

"You will?" Karolena asked at the same time as Jordan.

He nodded. "With one condition."

"There's always a fucking catch," Aarav muttered between sips of his tea.

"There's a man. His name is Konstantin. You need to take him with you. Keep him safe until I can come for him." Steel returned to Levin's spine and to his stare. "If even one hair on his head is harmed, we're done. I'm out."

"That seems fair enough." Jordan nodded.

"Who is he?" Karolena asked, drawing a blank as she cycled through all of Vladimir's higher-ups that she knew and came up blank.

"He's one of the brigadiers." By that he meant an officer in Vladimir's army. "And he's my boyfriend."

"Ah, fuck." Tavish groaned.

Karolena didn't think it was possible to be more shocked than she'd already been that afternoon. "Really?"

"Yes. At least I'd like him to be. But things are... complicated, given the situation. Still, he's the one responsible for making me realize how fucked up my life is. Not to mention the impact of the things I've done, like recruiting others into the organization. Regardless of if he wants to stay with me when he no longer has to, I'm set on getting him out. To give him back his life. I'd risk everything for that."

Aven sighed and fanned herself faster.

Karolena's eyes stung as she considered the man in front of her. Was he perfect? Of course not. Was he deserving of a chance to atone for his mistakes? She thought so.

"We'll take care of your Konstantin," James promised.

"You remind me of him a bit." Levin turned away then until he could get himself under control. Karolena hugged him from behind as she shot a glare at Tavish and Legend, daring them to say one damn word about offering her friend comfort.

"Okay, then." Jordan went into focus mode. "Let's hammer out how we're going to get this done."

"If you don't need me anymore, I think I'll leave you to work out the details." Karolena edged toward the door.

"Where are you going?" Tavish asked.

She resisted the urge to give him the finger. "Upstairs, to do my job. I'm sure there's something that needs to be cleaned since that's all it seems I'm good for around here."

"Oh fuck, now I know she's really mad." Aven frowned.

"Karolena..." When Tavish rose, Legend grabbed hold of his kilt and yanked him back down.

"Not now." Legend shook his head. "She asked for space. Give it to her. Respect her boundaries. It's the least we can do."

"Go ahead." Jordan smiled ruefully at her. "I'm so sorry about your mother. And for having to be strict under these circumstances. I hope you'll give us another chance to show you that you're important to us, and not only because of this stuff."

"All I can promise is that I'm going to take some time to reflect. And scrub the hell out of something. And rack up your bill with that therapist."

"You do that." Jordan tapped his pen on the table.

Levin beamed, as if he liked the woman she'd turned

into in such a short time. Who would she be in another week, or even a year?

What did she want for herself? Did it include a relationship with a man—or two—who might never truly be sure of her?

That's what she intended to figure out.

15

———

Legend watched Karolena's retreating form until she turned the corner toward the bank of elevators. It took every speck of self-control he had not to dash after her and beg her not to dump his ass. Or his boyfriend's.

He snarled at Tavish. "You idiot!"

"Not now." Jordan's mouth was a slash across his handsome face. "Remember what happened last time two of you started fighting over a woman when we should have been focused?"

"I do." Ruby glared at Ace and Liam. "We're not doing that again."

"All I have to say is that you better get your shit together and make this right." Levin planted his fists on the table and leaned in to glare at them. "I didn't save her from that asshole just for you two to play with her then toss her aside like your trash."

"That's not what's happening." Legend held his hands up. "Tavish has issues. We're working on it."

Jordan hummed. "Good."

"Before we get started again..." Legend turned to Aven. "If it's okay with Jordan, would you make a personal flight for me when we're done here? I have some ideas about how to fix this."

"How long would it take?" Jordan asked, his brows raised.

"An hour? Maybe two?"

"Sure, that's fine with me." Jordan nodded. "As long as she has enough time for a full night's sleep. We're going to need her to fly all day tomorrow."

"Would you be up for that? I'll pay you myself, of course." Legend was prepared to beg. He knew it was going to take something substantial to repair the damage Tavish had done, whether he could help it or not.

"Wow, am I hearing this right?" Sola teased him. "Mr. Save-All-My-Pennies-For-A-Rainy-Day wants to splurge? On a woman?"

"It will be a damn rainy day if she doesn't understand how important she is to me. To us."

Tavish dropped his face into his hands. "Please help so I don't fuck this up entirely."

"It might already be too late." Levin frowned. "She wasn't mad, she was hurt. And she's had enough of that in her life already. Fix it."

"So yeah, I'll do whatever it takes. Spend whatever it costs—money or my pride, it doesn't matter." Legend shrugged.

Jordan sighed. "You know I hate thinking about the past, but sometimes you have to enjoy the sun while it's shining. Because when the real stormy days do come, you want to know you took advantage of every chance you had to make the people who matter happy."

Legend understood Jordan was referring to his first

love. His partner at ICE, who'd been killed on the job. Bled out in his arms. He and Wren had nearly lost each other after that.

"Especially us," Liam piled on. He would. After Ace had been wounded in the field, he'd been terrified of getting too invested in a relationship with his partner but he'd overcome his fears, with Ruby's help.

"I get it." Legend truly did. Before they headed to Russia in the morning, he was going to have to make sure they left on good terms with Karolena.

Legend looked to Tavish, who nodded then hung his head. "I'm sorry I screwed this up for you too."

"Just make it right." Legend was relieved Tavish wasn't backing away entirely. It had been a reflexive instinct to protect his heart even if that was no longer necessary. Not with him and not with Karolena.

"What do you have in mind?" Tavish asked.

He conveyed his vision and counted on his friends to help bring it to life. James fired off a bunch of texts and assured him everything would be taken care of while Aven filed a flight plan. It was things like this that helped carry them through their more somber duties.

By the time they were done, even Levin cracked a smile.

Jordan turned his attention to more serious matters. "Let's get back to this."

"You're proving I'm doing the right thing here." Levin drew a deep breath. "This is the kind of place I thought our organization was once. One I would have liked to belong to, if things had been different."

"Things can always be different." Tavish shocked the hell out of Legend when he said it, reaching over to rest his hand on Legend's leg beneath the table. "When you find the right people, everything changes. For the better. As long as you don't forget and fuck it up by being stuck in the past."

"We'll fix it," Legend promised.

"After," Jordan said, then instructed Ruby to pull up a map of Vladimir's compound.

Then they concentrated on ensuring that their woman and her friend and his man would have a chance to build futures like the one they finally had within reach.

16

———

Legend studied himself in the mirror and adjusted the bow tie of his tux one final time.

"You look hot as fuck," Tavish promised from the doorway. "Come on, Aven could be back any minute. We don't want to miss her."

When Legend spun to face his roommate, he froze. "Shit, you look good too. I've never seen you wear all that before."

"It's a traditional kilt. Much more formal." A white tuxedo shirt and black bowtie was covered by a vest, then by a Prince Charlie jacket with six silver buttons on the body and another three on the lower half of each sleeve. A chain draped around Tavish's waist left a fur sporran to draw Legend's eyes to the front center of the blue-and-black tartan, another piece of which was pinned over Tavish's left shoulder. It draped down his back like a plaid cape. A small knife tucked in the top of his matching hose seemed rather appropriate and matched his shiny black leather shoes. His hair was neat and slicked into a man

177

bun that Legend fantasized about grabbing hold of while they were making out.

Tavish grinned as he noticed the bulge in Legend's dress pants. They hid nothing.

If they didn't leave right then, they were going to screw up their hard work and carefully laid plains. They'd spent the past two hours that Aven had been flying setting everything else into motion with the help of their friends.

"What if it's not enough?" Tavish asked. "What if she doesn't believe that I'm trying my best and that my reaction had nothing to do with her and everything to do with me?"

"We'll figure it out if it comes to that, but I think it might help if you promise her you'll start going to therapy like she does. I swear she's made more progress in a week than you have since...the incident."

Tavish grunted. "Yeah. Okay. I want that for myself too, you know?"

"I think that will matter a lot. It does to me." Legend hugged Tavish, proud of him for admitting his flaws and seeking help, no matter how long it had taken. It wasn't often they embraced without intent to do more but he hoped maybe they could form a new, healthier habit.

They left the apartment together, headed for Karolena's next door, which she'd only slept in once, that first night. He hoped she wouldn't ever again either because he'd gotten used having her in his bed. Legend rapped on the door, a bit louder than he'd intended.

From inside he heard a curse then a crack.

"Karolena? Everything okay?" He called, prepared to kick down the door if she didn't provide him reassurance.

Instead, the thing was whipped open. She didn't step aside to let them in, leveling a hostile stare in their direction as she clutched her poor mop, now split in two. She must have been putting all her weight on it as she scrubbed furiously to have it fail her like that.

"Of course it's not." She flailed with the broken mop, making him take a step back to avoid getting whacked. She tried to peer around them, but they blocked the entire doorway and then some. "Where's Levin? *How* is he?"

"He's still working with Jordan and Ruby on transferring intel. He's fine, though. Jordan offered him a break to sleep but he knows our time is limited so he's trying to communicate as much as possible while he can speak openly."

Karolena nodded. "I told you he was decent. Relatively."

"We should have believed you." It was only one of many mistakes they'd made, which he intended to correct. It was then she seemed to notice their clothes.

"Where are you going?" Karolena asked as she checked them over, not at all subtly. Her hungry assessment gave him some hope that she might not send them away without hearing them out.

"On a date." Legend fiddled with his bowtie again.

"Oh." Her face fell and she began to shut the door. Did she think they'd lied about seeing other people too? Damn it.

Legend slapped his palm on it and elbowed Tavish, who sputtered. "With you, Karolena. We hope."

She stopped forcing the door closed, then narrowed her eyes at them for a few moments.

"I'd say I don't want to go anywhere with you, but we both know that's a lie even if it makes me stupid." She tossed the halves of the broken mop onto the floor, disgusted.

"You're not dumb." He grasped her hand, hoping to reassure both of them. "We'd like a chance to make up for earlier, even if we don't deserve it."

"I'm prepared to grovel." Tavish drew a cross over his heart.

She looked at the splintered pieces at their feet and the sparkling though stark apartment surrounding her, then down at her uniform. "I'm in no state to go out. Besides, I doubt Jordan or Levin would let me anyway."

"None of that matters where we're headed." Legend raised her so he could kiss her fingers. "You can come as you are. If you want, we've arranged something fancy for you to wear too."

"You have?" Despite her residual ire, she perked up a bit at that.

Legend had the urge to chuckle, but knew better.

On the other hand, Tavish didn't. "Yeah. Let us spoil you tonight, please?"

"I'm not sure I'm up for all that." She sighed. "But I'm willing to attempt a civil conversation. Would we be able to talk on this date?"

"Absolutely." Legend nodded. "That's the plan."

Karolena took a moment to decide. His heart pounded as he waited for the verdict.

"Fine, but if I change my mind you'll need to bring me home right away. No arguments." She crossed her arms. He loved that she was setting healthy boundaries and learning to be assertive despite how unused to it she was.

"Of course." It was an easy promise to make. Tavish nodded too.

When he gestured for her to step out with them, she did and headed for the elevators. Unlike all the other times they'd done that, he pushed the up button instead of down. Karolena raised a questioning gaze to him. "Where are we going?"

"We still don't have any real balconies at Shields, but we do have a roof." Tavish entered the elevator. He held the doors for her and Legend then hit the button for the top floor.

Karolena's eyes sparkled in the halogen lights. Legend was sure she appreciated an adventure and made note to take her on plenty in the future, if she'd let them.

When they were let out on the top floor, they had to take one final industrial-looking cement-and-metal stairway to the roof. The door had extra security that he cleared with a fingerprint scanner. When he held his hand to Karolena, she took it, so he led her outside, where their helipad occupied a portion of the space.

In the corner as far away from it as possible, an oasis of artificial turf was surrounded by oversized brushed nickel lanterns. Beveled glass sheltered the flames of zillions of candles. Strands of bistro lights with round bulbs were strung in long arcs between elevated poles that defined the rooftop retreat. Inside the area, a square wooden table with formal chairs on three sides sat diagonal from a canopied daybed. They'd swapped the heavy canvas curtains on it for mosquito netting to lend it an airy touch with the illusion of privacy that still allowed its occupants to stargaze while lounging on it.

Fresh flowers overflowed vases set on pedestals of varying heights between the lanterns. White heirloom roses and peonies nestled among unique greenery he didn't even know the name of. Didn't need to, to be impressed by how gorgeous and sophisticated it all looked.

Beside the bouquet at the center of the table, an

ornate silver bucket held ice and a very expensive bottle of champagne. Three crystal flutes cast rainbows onto the table from the candlelight shining through them.

"You had this up here the whole time and you're just telling me now?" Karolena went straight over to examine their handiwork. "This is incredible."

"Actually, no." Legend shook his head.

Tavish stepped in front of her at the entrance to the getaway. He took her hands in his and waited until she met his gaze before admitting, "The Shields and our other Middletown friends set this up to help us convince you that you're special to us, even if we're works in progress. I'm so sorry I got triggered earlier and that my insecurities came to the surface. It had nothing to do with you, Karolena, and everything to do with my past."

Karolena sniffled, looking between him and Legend and then back to the open-air space. "You really did this for me?"

"Of course." Legend joined them, putting his hands over hers and Tavish's where they were joined. "And it's only a small demonstration of what we would like to do for you. You're good for us, Karolena. You make us tackle these difficult conversations and be honest about what we need from each other, because with you, I think we might finally have a shot at finding something we never thought we'd have. Everlasting joy."

A tear rolled down her check and he couldn't help but lean in and kiss it away.

"I think it hurt so much because I feel the same way and I've never had anything I was afraid of losing before." Karolena looked back at what they'd made for her. "How the hell did you pull this off?"

"It doesn't hurt having lots of helping hands." Tavish

smiled. "Plus Laurel and Kate have the home décor business, which came in clutch. Joe and Morgan had a lot of suggestions too. I guess he wooed her with a private dinner in a pumpkin patch once. If it worked for him..."

"Is it going to work for us too?" Legend asked, afraid to hope.

Before Karolena could respond, the familiar *wop wop wop* of an approaching helicopter cut through the night. Legend and Tavish bundled Karolena between them as the lights grew brighter. Legend said, "Duck your face, it's going to get windy."

Thankfully the lanterns did their jobs and the flowers didn't seem too disturbed as the chopper touched down, light as a feather, and its engine cut out.

"What—?" Karolena looked to them until the pilot's door opened and Aven waved.

The three of them crossed to the helicopter.

"I believe I have a delivery for you, ma'am." She reached over and retrieved a black bag with a foiled gold logo from the passenger seat and handed it down to Karolena, followed by a shoebox.

She took one look at the packages and gasped. "These are my favorite designers."

"Levin told us." Tavish flashed her a wry smile. "I guess he's good for something, huh?"

Legend braced himself, but Karolena laughed and swung the bag at Tavish, making Legend feel lighter than he had since that morning when the foundation for their future with her had nearly gone up in flames at least as devastating as the ones the Heat had unleashed on James's car.

"You really believe me about him?" she asked Tavish.

"I do. I could clearly see the difference between the

way he talked about his *sestra* and his boyfriend. And even if I hadn't, your reaction told me that I'd fucked up. My heart knew even if my brain refused to believe. I'm scared to get this wrong and yet somehow I still did."

"That hasn't really sunk in yet. Everything he shared." Karolena seemed a bit dazed as she looked from the clothes in her hands to the helicopter and then to the rooftop patio.

Aven reached into the back and started hauling out additional bags. "There's more. These two had me hit up the best five-star restaurant in the closest big city, where that fancy-ass boutique was. I've got seven courses of your favorite foods here too. Want me to help you get changed and do something with your hair while these two get dinner ready?"

"I would love that." Karolena wiped another tear from her cheek. Hopefully this time a happy one. "Thank you."

She shifted her gaze from Aven, to Legend, then Tavish.

"If you let us, we'll try to make as many of your days happy ones as possible, Karolena." Legend couldn't help but steal a gentle kiss before collecting the food from Aven and leaving the women alone so he and Tavish could unpack it onto the fancy dishes Devra had set out on the buffet along one wall of the roof.

It wasn't more than ten minutes before they'd tucked the last of the containers out of sight under a tablecloth and Tavish froze, staring in the direction of stairwell the women had disappeared into.

Legend spun around and got stuck too.

Karolena strode toward them with a confidence she'd never possessed before. It was the most attractive thing he'd ever seen. He could imagine her as a model, tall and thin in killer heels that made her legs look even longer than they were. Her hair was swept off her face and clipped in an updo that allowed wisps to frame her face. And that dress...whatever obscene amount of money they'd charged to his credit card had been worth it.

The floor-length skirt was slit nearly to her hipbone, giving him glimpses of her svelte thigh between the floaty, black fabric as she walked. The top was a deep v that plunged nearly to her navel, leaving two points of fabric over her breasts. They were held in place by ultra-thin straps that he would guess crisscrossed her bare back. A glittering belt of rhinestones emphasized her tiny waist.

"I'm going downstairs," Aven shouted to them from the doorway. "You look gorgeous! Kiss and make up, please."

Legend shot her a salute. Tavish grinned. They each held out a hand to Karolena as she approached, and she accepted them.

"She's right, you know?" Legend could hardly speak. "You're amazing."

"I feel more like myself." Karolena ducked her head as if she was kind of embarrassed by her high maintenance tendencies. "No, more like the woman I want to be. Desirable, and in control of my own destiny."

"You're both of those things." Tavish wrapped his hand around her elbow and led her to the table. Legend drew her chair out and held it steady as Tavish settled her then tucked her in.

Legend retrieved the trio of appetizers from the sideboard and set one at each of their places while Tavish poured them champagne. Despite everything, Karolena hesitated just long enough that Legend caught it. "Don't you believe us? I understand if it takes time to earn back your trust."

She sighed. "Look me straight in the face and swear that this isn't only some assignment to you. Promise we're not playing some game I don't know the rules of. Because if you are, that's more cruel than anything Vladimir did to me. At least he was honest and direct about his intentions."

Tavish didn't balk. He took her hand and swore it. "Everything that's happened between us and what I hope will come next is because we want you for you. You're courageous, and stronger than you realize. And so damn sexy."

"Plus, you brought Tavish and I together far more tightly than we had managed on our own." Legend cleared his throat. "I'm starting to think I might not lose him. That someday, he might come to love me the way I love him."

"I've always loved you." Tavish looked at Legend like he'd said Aven's chopper was an alien spaceship. "How could you not know?"

"Because you're too afraid to show it. Maybe even to admit to yourself how desperately you need him." Karolena squeezed his fingers. "You're going to have to learn to open yourself to more than sex if you want to keep him."

"Fuck." Tavish groaned. "I already told him I'm going to be more like you and tackle my shit head on. I'll make a therapy appointment as soon as we get inside. I don't want my shit to come back on you two ever again. I'm so sorry." This time he apologized to Legend and not Karolena.

"I forgive you," Legend promised.

"And so do I." Karolena looked to them both. "Can we

eat? I haven't had anything all day and this smells so delicious I'm drooling."

"Me too." But Legend was still looking at his companions and not their plates.

Fuck the food.

"Save that look for after dessert." Karolena refused to budge. "I'm not letting one crumb of this dinner go to waste. Waiter, my napkin please."

"Of course, my lady." Tavish unfurled the white linen and set it across her lap. "Would you like me to feed it to you too?"

Legend groaned when Tavish forked up a bit and slipped it between Karolena's lips, causing her to hum at the flavor. This was going to be a long couple of hours and nothing was going to appease his appetite before he consumed Karolena and Tavish.

17

Karolena licked the back of her spoon, then set it on the pretty plate with the thin gold edge, her taste buds and her heart singing. The past several hours had been such a welcome break, a relief from the stress that had been wringing her guts since the instant she'd seen Levin strolling along Middletown's sidewalk.

For the evening, she'd been able to pretend that tomorrow might never come. That she and Legend and Tavish could stay there with only the sky above, no ceiling, forever. Their laughter and deep conversation, hopes and dreams for the future, plus praise for the exquisite meal, had filled the night air.

Not one of them had rushed, as if they each expected they'd have a lifetime to spend with each other. Of course, that might not be possible, even if they wished it was.

Legend picked up her plate along with his and Tavish's and stacked them neatly on the rest. He put the silverware in a basket and moaned. "Who's going to do all the dishes?"

"Well, it's probably my job." She shrugged one shoulder. "Besides, it's the least I can do after you two and everyone else went to so much trouble for me."

"We'll always do our best for you," he said quietly as he returned to her side.

Instead of reclaiming his seat, he held out his hand and helped her to her feet. He wrapped her in a hug that made her feel as secure as if Vladimir were on the moon instead of still part of their world. "All I ask is that you come back to me."

"That's one thing we can't promise," Tavish murmured as he came up behind her and kissed the nape of her neck. "But I tell you this: I will do everything in my power to protect Legend when we're on a mission."

"I'm glad we shared this tonight and talked things through. I never want to leave with things uneasy between us. Just in case..." Legend swayed a bit, cradling her, and Tavish followed along until they were nearly slow dancing in the flickering candlelight.

She thought about how someday, they could be used up, just like her mop. A tool for governments and all of humanity—even those who never knew Shields existed—that had served its purpose and been worn out. Or have a not-so-accident, like her mother's.

There were things she'd never get to say to the woman who'd raised her. They'd been robbed of time they should have spent together.

Karolena would never let that happen to her again. "If this could be one of our last nights together, I don't want to waste it."

"The point of all this wasn't to seduce you." Legend brushed stray tendrils from her face.

"But if that's a bonus...I'm not going to say no to

testing out that bed over there." Tavish kissed her shoulder, making her shiver.

Legend rubbed her arms. Did she have the guts to be as forthright as she'd demanded of them? To admit what she really craved in that moment? "If you truly trust me, both of you, then I want you to show me what it's like when you make love to each other. While I watch."

"Should I bend him over right here on this table for old times' sake?" Tavish asked in her ear, letting her feel how hard he'd gotten at her request when he rubbed up against her ass.

Legend stiffened in front of her, but not in the same way. She understood immediately.

She called Tavish on his bad habits. "Absolutely not. I didn't say anything about fucking. I want you to be as romantic with him as you were with me when you did all of this. He deserves that from you." Karolena swept her arm around, gesturing at the flowers and lights and the fantasy they'd brought to life for her.

Legend sucked in a breath, holding it as Tavish digested her wish.

And when Tavish took one of their hands in each of his and walked backward toward the canopied bed, they went—very willingly—with him.

When they reached it, he drew the netting aside and revealed a carved wooden box on the center of the mattress.

"What's that?" Legend asked.

"No idea. I thought you put it there." Tavish picked it up.

The three of them watched as he opened it. There was a note on top that said, *With love, for love. ~Your friends.*

Inside, on a red velvet lining, was a bottle of lube, a

pair of handcuffs, and some gadget that she assumed was a vibrator though she'd never seen the sort before.

Tavish beamed. "They really did think of everything, huh?"

He placed it carefully at the foot of the bed then turned back to Legend and Karolena. "Anyone need help getting out of these get ups?"

Karolena spun so her back was to him and nodded. "Will you untie me, please?"

"I might rather tie you up, but we can save that for another time." His voice rasped in her ear as he released the knot at the back of her neck, causing the entire front of her dress to fall away.

Legend blew out a breath as he took in the sight of her standing before him in the moonlight. "You don't mind being naked while we're dressed?"

Funny, she hadn't even thought of it. "It's not making me anxious, but I do want to see you. And touch you, once Tavish is done having his way with you."

Legend bent to untie his dress shoes, then started to strip even as Tavish slipped her dress down to her ankles and helped her step out of it. She stood there for a moment in only her heels, very aware of his stare on every bare inch of her body.

"That image will be burned in my memory forever." He dragged his fingers down her spine, then lower until he crouched to slip her shoes from her feet. Tavish scooped her up and carried her to the bed, laying her on the pile of cushions at the top.

He snagged the toy from the box and handed it to her. "Feel free to play with this while you watch."

"How?" Her cheeks flushed as she admitted how little she knew about things they were experts in.

Tavish took the hollow oval on the front of it and placed it over her clit before pressing the button on the handle. When it came to life with a quiet hum, it felt like he was sucking on her. "Oh."

He chuckled and Legend groaned. "Yeah. I prefer to do it myself, but sometimes it's convenient to have some help while I'm otherwise occupied."

Karolena didn't waste any time. She tested out various angles and speeds while Legend finished removing his tux and started in on Tavish's kilt, helping him unpin his tartan and slip out of the handsome jacket hugging his fit torso.

And when Legend bent to remove Tavish's hose and shoes, carefully setting his knife aside, Tavish made quick work of the buckles holding the bottom half of his outfit in place. That left Legend's face at cock level.

Tavish didn't demand Legend suck him. But Legend did it anyway.

He tipped Tavish's cock toward his mouth and took it between his lips, sliding down to the base with a single greedy gulp that had Tavish cursing. He let Legend have his way for a few minutes, standing feet spread, hand fisted in Legend's hair as he let his partner do his best.

When Karolena turned the speed of the vibrator up a notch, he smiled at her and tapped Legend's shoulder, pointing to the space at her feet. He put a hand below Legend's arm and helped him rise though he didn't need assistance.

The men kissed, their mouths a bit harsh where they clashed and parried with each other.

And when they tumbled to the bed together, Karolena bounced.

They were even more beautiful when they were like this, raw and open with each other.

After taking his fill of Legend's lips, Tavish spun around. He rolled Legend to his back and straddled his head, facing the other man's feet, so that he could feed Legend his cock once again. Only this time, he didn't stop there. He tipped forward so that he could return the favor.

At first he curled his hand around Legend's shaft, pumping until a shimmery bead of fluid appeared at the tip. He didn't waste it. Tavish dipped his head and lapped it from the fat head of Legend's cock before swallowing as much of Legend as he could. It was more than she had managed but still not nearly all of him.

Legend didn't seem to mind. He reached up and clasped Tavish's ass, even as Tavish moved over Legend with the grace of a powerful animal. His muscles flexed and rippled in the lights that danced around them.

Karolena felt herself tightening and wished one—or both—of them was buried inside her while the toy worked its magic. She must have made a noise because both men peered at her as best they could from their stations.

Their eyes on her while their mouths were on each other's cocks, plus the rhythmic suction of the vibrator set her off. She came as she threw her head back, the stars twinkling above her matching the pleasure that sparkled throughout her entire body.

Tavish pulled away from Legend, leaving all three of them panting. Legend wiped his mouth, then said, "I need a minute. That was…"

"Sexy as hell." Tavish ringed the base of his slick shaft as if to keep himself from erupting. "You're incredible, Karolena."

"Me?" She tried not to be too embarrassed. "I didn't even do anything."

"I'll never get tired of watching you come." He leaned over to kiss her, fierce and possessive, like he had been with Legend. That meant something to her. To them, she wasn't broken or icy or lacking in any way.

Karolena returned his kiss but pulled away when she thought he might forget their purpose. She whispered, "Fuck our man, Tavish. He needs you."

"He needs *us*," Tavish corrected.

"I need somebody." Legend stroked his own cock. "Don't leave me over here by myself."

Tavish knelt in front of Legend. He took his cock and smacked it against Legend's a few times. Then he reached around Legend, squeezing his ass as he demanded, "Get over there and do a better job than her new friend. I'm going to open this up while you do."

Legend practically dove for Karolena, encouraging her to spread her legs wider to accommodate his broad shoulders. He slid his hands beneath her ass and fit her to his face, wasting no time in lapping up the slickness from her recent orgasm.

Her body still hummed like a tuning fork that had been struck and left to ring out. So when he applied every skill he had to enhancing those resonances, it didn't take long for her to reach a fevered pitch again.

Tavish added to her crescendoing arousal when he slicked his fingers with lube and slipped them between Legend's cheeks, pressing them to his ass. Legend groaned against her flesh, sharing the impact of Tavish's touch with her. She stared, fascinated, as Tavish increased the pressure until finally Legend relaxed enough to let him penetrate.

Tavish probed deeper as he caressed Legend's flank with his free hand.

"What does that feel like?" Karolena wondered.

Tavish snatched her hand from Legend's shoulder. He slathered her fingers in lube, stroking them a few times until the gel lost its coolness. Then he encouraged her to sit forward a bit and guided her to Legend's hole. It was a bit of a stretch, but she could barely reach.

After checking to make sure she was comfortable, Tavish nudged her so she would press in beside him. Her first attempt didn't do the trick.

Legend shoved backward against them when she was too timid, afraid of hurting him. He licked her faster and a bit more erratically as her digits sank into him beside Tavish's.

"Hot and tight." She moaned as he clenched around her, pressing her tighter to Tavish's hand, which was gliding in and out.

"It feels so good when my dick is in here. I can't wait to get inside this ass." Tavish sounded a bit strangled now.

"But that's mostly because it is *this* ass, right?" Karolena didn't intend to let Tavish off the hook or resort to bad habits. "It feels better because it's Legend letting you fuck him and you admire him so much."

"Of course." Tavish looked at her like she had lost it. "He knows that."

"I'm not sure he does." She peered into Legend's eyes then and saw the doubt and hope there.

Tavish paused. "You do know that, don't you?"

Legend still didn't respond, so Tavish pushed his fingers fully within Legend, who never stopped eating her.

"Ah, Legend. I'm so sorry I haven't said so before. That I couldn't." Tavish leaned forward and kissed Legend's shoulder, then the spot in between them. His other hand snaked around Legend's hip and stroked his cock in time to the pumps of their now synchronized fingers in the other man's ass. "It means so much to me that you let me in. You're the best man I know. Selfless, dauntless, and an absolute warrior. I'm so lucky you're my partner in the field and off of it."

The relief and ecstasy of an entirely different sort that lit up Legend's face set Karolena off. She arched beneath them, her fingers slipping from Legend, as she cried out into the night.

From far away, through a fog of rapture, she heard Tavish command Legend, "Move up. Give her that big fat dick of yours. Kiss her, hold her, fuck her, and let me do the same to you. We're going to surround you and give you as much of us as you can stand."

Legend moaned but didn't do as Tavish told him right away. Karolena forced her eyes open to see what the holdup was. He was staring down at her, the corners of his mouth pinched.

"You don't have to if you don't want to." She was content to share in their experience however they saw fit.

"If I do that, I'll be on top of you. And him on me." Legend drew a meandering path down her center from her collarbones to her pussy. "I would love it, but not if it makes you uncomfortable."

It surprised her when she realized that not only had she not recoiled in anticipation of being trapped, pinned under both of the men, but she also was looking forward to the weight and heat of them on her. "Somehow it's not frightening when it's you. Earlier, I felt like I had lost you. Or maybe never even truly had you."

"Damn it." Tavish practically shook with self-recrimination. It wasn't her intention to punish them, but she needed them to understand.

"Imprint yourselves on every inch of me. Make me feel like I belong to you both." Karolena took Legend's shoulders in her hands and drew him to her.

"I can promise you that we belong to you." Tavish took Legend's cock in one fist and his balls in the other. He used the delicate grip to guide his best friend to Karolena. "Go ahead, Legend. Give her what all three of us want."

It still took a bit of maneuvering to work him into her, no matter how turned on she was, but they ground on each other until he sank inside bit by bit.

"That's right. Almost there. All the way, Legend. Then hold still for me."

Legend obeyed, kissing Karolena with long, gentle sweeps of his lips when words failed them both. She held him tight, reveling in the full-body contact. Skin on skin, she hugged him within her as tightly as she embraced him with her arms.

And when Tavish finished slicking his cock, he joined them in a chain of desire and joy that she couldn't imagine ever breaking. Legend shook his head from side to side as he tried to absorb everything Tavish was giving him while they were locked together.

Tavish must have bottomed out in Legend because his forward momentum transferred through the other man and caused Legend to drive deeper into her. Karolena cried out Tavish's name.

He might have tried to smile reassurance at her, but instead his teeth were bared as he clung to what self-restraint he had. Karolena moaned when he blanketed Legend's back long enough to catch her mouth for a quick kiss before relinquishing her lips to Legend once more.

And when he straightened up again, he began to move.

He lunged over them slowly at first, though it wasn't long before he picked up the pace and force with which he seated himself inside Legend over and over. It wasn't a sexual marathon like some of the times they'd come together, but the truth was, none of them could withstand passion that intense for long.

Bliss mixed with affection to form a combination so potent, resisting its effect was futile.

"Karolena! Tavish!" Legend roared. "It's too good."

"No, it's perfect." Tavish smacked his ass once, hard. Then he studied Karolena as if judging how close she was. She nodded at him, clinging to the razor's edge of rapture as their pleasure drove her own.

Legend warned, "If you don't stop—"

"You're going to fill her pussy up?" Tavish shoved him over the edge with his filthy mouth. "Come so hard you wring every last drop of come from my balls with your sweet ass?"

"Yeah. That." Legend drew so tight, his muscles coiled, that Tavish essentially used him to fuck her too. Every slap of his torso on Legend's ass shoved Legend's cock into her.

But it was the desperate cry that Legend gave when he surrendered, emptying himself within her that triggered her own orgasm. Its power shocked her, though not enough to become oblivious to Tavish, who launched into a flurry of frantic strokes before pumping his own release deep into Legend.

After the first tsunami of rapture hit them all, it was followed by gradually lessening waves they rode with slow grinds and flexes. Only when Legend's cock softened enough that he slipped from her pussy did he shift and Tavish with him.

They ended up lying on either side of her, boneless as they floated while staring up at the stars. Karolena let her worries drift away as she contemplated her place in the universe and how lucky she'd been to wind up there, on a rooftop in the middle of a town she'd never known existed, happier than she'd ever dreamed she could be.

A long time later, Tavish reached for the blanket at the foot of the bed. "Are you cold?"

"Between the two of you?" She huffed out a laugh. "Not possible."

Still, he drew up the cover and tucked them in together.

Legend still hadn't budged. She laid her cheek on his chest and patted it. "What are you thinking about?"

He shook his head as if it was nothing, but the furrow of his brow made her sure it was something.

"We made Tavish come clean, so you should too." She raked her teeth over his nipple, making him jerk.

"Just thinking how much more critical things are now than on some random mission. And they're already pretty steep then." He sighed. "I've never wanted to come home to something so badly before."

Karolena's heart skipped a beat. If she were only an assignment to them they wouldn't give a shit about what happened after it was over. But he was right. Her piece of shit ex wasn't someone to mess with. Suddenly she did need the blanket after all.

"Maybe he's already forgotten about me. He has bigger things to worry about."

"You have no idea how special you are. Even now."

Tavish stroked his fingers through her hair. "Don't worry, I hope we'll have a long, long time to show you."

"Seriously, though..." Karolena lost a bit of her buzz. "He's evil and without qualms. He'll cut you down without a second thought."

Legend rolled onto his side so he could peer down at her. "Tavish trusted us. Now you need to have some faith in him and me. We've taken down plenty of fuckers as bad as Vladimir or worse. We'll eliminate this problem for you, permanently, even if it is the last thing we do."

"It would be worth it to ensure your safety for good even if we weren't around to share it with you," Tavish agreed.

"Not to me."

"Let's not think about that tonight. Morning's coming soon enough. I don't want to deal with it until we leave at first light." Legend nuzzled his nose against her cheek.

Karolena stiffened. "So soon?"

"Vladimir will be expecting his soldier back. We're going to have to move quickly," Tavish informed her. She should have considered that but they'd occupied her every thought.

"And come back to me just as fast?" She hated being needy.

"You still don't think we're serious about you?" Legend tipped his head.

"No, you convinced me of that. Now I'm afraid I won't be able to handle it if something happens to either of you, especially if it's because of me."

"This is because of him, not you. Never forget that. You didn't ask for this," Tavish reminded her.

"I finally feel like I belong somewhere. I don't want to

lose this too." Karolena choked back tears. Legend was right, her whole soul was at stake.

Tavish tripped up a bit. "This is why you don't get serious."

Legend kept him from spiraling into his old pattern of thinking. "No, this is why you don't fuck around. Because life is too short to waste on not going all in."

For the first time, Karolena feared she might have been wrong and exposed all three of them to irreparable heartbreak.

As usual, Legend held strong. "If we don't come home, Shields will still look out for you. No one's kicking you out, okay? It's fair to say we're still dealing with our shit and will be for some time. As long as we're prepared to work on it—and take these leaps of faith together, even when we're terrified—I can live with that."

"I'll jump with you anytime." Tavish kissed Legend and then her.

Karolena wasn't sure it was the smartest thing she'd ever done, but it might have been the most courageous. She whispered, "I'm in."

They held each other under the canopy of stars, breathing deep of the pine scent and listening to the hooting of owls in the distance as they spent what could be their final hours together in each other's arms. For the moment, in harmony.

18

───────

Tavish slumped in one of the oversized leather captain's chairs of the Shields' private jet, still fuming as Aven launched them into the air. He'd never been furious during a briefing before.

"Shake it off." Legend leaned in. "Every detail is important. We can't miss a single one just because we're pissed."

"I'm aware." Tavish glared at Levin, who occupied the seat across from him in the cluster of four that faced each other, next to Karolena.

Karolena. With them, on the jet, headed back to Russia.

"*Sestra's* not going to be in any danger at all." Levin repeated himself for the millionth time. "I wouldn't agree to that any more than you would."

"Clearly, that's not true." Tavish wished they'd shot the bastard on sight. "Private airfield or not, she'd be better protected at Shields."

"It's okay, guys." Karolena leaned forward to rub Tavish's knee. "Levin had a point. Konstantin will have no reason to trust the Shields without someone he knows to explain what's going on. Levin's not going to have time to tell him everything, and each minute longer you stay there, the more likely it is for you to get caught. Konstantin will either be a burden, trying to fight you off, or need to be restrained until you could get him all the way to headquarters. That's cruel."

"Plus, he's a resourceful fucker." Levin flashed an indulgent and proud smile. "I wouldn't be surprised if he got loose and took a few of you out before trying to land this thing himself. Probably not wise on a jet over open ocean."

"I swear, my ass will be planted right here in this seat. I will not budge to so much as peek out the door to see if you're on your way back yet." Karolena had been awfully eager to return. Tavish repeated over and over that it was because she was worried for him and Legend, not because she and Levin were planning some coup.

Twelve hours of flight time was going to vanish fast between rehearsing their plan, devising fallback strategies, and undertaking and analysis of potential pitfalls. Tavish drew a deep breath and peered around at the other agents on the flight. Kennedy would also be staying on the plane. Hopefully, they wouldn't need her medic services. Nolan, Marcus, and Knox would guard it, ensuring their safe passage out of hostile territory and the safety of Aven, Kennedy, and Karolena.

"It better be," Tavish grumbled.

Legend kicked his boot. Tavish shut up before he said something he'd regret.

Karolena peered out of the corner of her eye toward Levin, then said, "I'm glad Aven will keep me company while we're waiting for you to do your spy thing."

"You've become friends, yes?" Levin asked with just a hint of something Tavish couldn't quite place.

"She's great." Karolena nodded. "And I don't think she likes being alone any more than I do."

"Hmm." Levin stared at the cockpit. With the door open, he'd have a perfect view of Aven manning the controls. The ten thousand buttons up there gave Tavish a headache, but she seemed to work them like a conductor directing an orchestra. It was pretty fascinating to watch.

"I noticed she brought you *syrnikis* for breakfast. Dumb luck she knew your favorite?" Karolena was not as subtle as she thought. Then again, neither were Russian pancakes with his preferred blueberry topping.

"No. She and I spent some time talking last night after she assured me you were well and accepting of the apology from these two dumbasses." Levin smirked at Legend and Tavish, which did nothing to reduce Tavish's blood pressure. "I cooked for us. There were leftovers. She was being kind. That's all."

Legend cleared his throat. "Good. Because I'm pretty sure you told us we were hauling some dude out of here because he's your boyfriend."

"You have a boyfriend, don't you?" Levin looked between Tavish and Legend. "Plus a girlfriend, at least unless you do something to screw that up again."

"True." Tavish blinked. "I think I do. I hope..."

Karolena beamed at him. "You do."

"I can't wait to see what Kon thinks of you all and your relationships. Not to mention Aven." Levin's smile turned wolfish. "I have a feeling they're going to get along great."

Tavish should have kept his mouth shut, but he wasn't good at that. "Would you care if they did?"

"Not at all." Levin folded his hands over his

washboard abs. The man was cocky, but probably rightfully so. "No one's going to steal him from me."

Tavish wished he had that sort of unshakeable confidence.

Some of his irritation dissipated as he considered how freaked out the guy was going to be and the impact of even a single familiar face. Besides, it's not like they were turning around to drop Karolena off at this point, so he might as well make the most of it.

Distractions melted away as they strategized and prepped for their strike. The more surgical they could be, the quicker they could get in and out, the better their odds of success would be. Plus, then they could spend the entire flight home celebrating with Karolena.

It felt like an hour but had really been twelve when they touched down as smoothly as they had taken off. Midnight engulfed the plane as Aven shut down as many lights as possible and drove to the refueling station. She'd waste no time in getting the plane ready for takeoff again, then would wait at the top of the runway, prepared to go at a moment's notice.

With or without them.

Familiar adrenaline surged through Tavish's veins. He bumped fists with Legend, then turned to Karolena. True to her word, her ass was planted in her seat with her belt on as the rest of the agents engaged in a flurry of last-minute preparations.

Tavish checked his weapons for the millionth time, then stole one quick but thorough kiss from Karolena before Legend did the same. "We'll see you soon."

"You'd better." She seemed to have utter faith in them, but when she turned to Levin, her lower lip wobbled. "Are you sure there's no other way?"

"Positive." He ruffled her hair. "Take care of my guy, *sestra*."

"I will." She put her hand over her heart, a lot passing between them with that simple gesture. "Be safe."

"I won't. But it has to be done." Levin stepped away then, putting space between them. "No matter what happens now, I don't regret the choices I've made. And if I go down trying to undo a system that I helped perpetuate, even if I didn't know any better, then at least it's in pursuit of something valuable instead of just more money or the illusion of power."

Kennedy flipped open a laptop. With a few keystrokes, she put a stream of the Shields' command center on a screen that descended from the ceiling in front of the bulkhead. Jordan stood with James by his side. Ruby manned the computers in the background. "Everyone's comms working?"

Tavish tapped his ear then nodded. Between their mics and body cams, the team would be able to watch as the mission went down. If something happened to him or Legend, Karolena would see it live. He prayed it didn't come to that.

Jordan gave the order. "Roll out."

Tavish sent Karolena one last piercing look, nodded, then jogged down the plane's stairs and across the tarmac to the black sedan waiting near the hangar.

Levin said he usually had a driver but had convinced Vladimir he didn't need one since he didn't know exactly when he'd be back and didn't care to wait for a ride. He popped the trunk but rather than loading baggage into it, he waved to Legend and Tavish.

"Is he going to fit in there?" Levin seemed skeptical.

"That's what she said." Tavish couldn't help himself.

Even in the most tense of situations, they could use a little levity.

Legend snorted as he folded himself into a bundle of muscle and retribution. "Drive fast so I don't get stuck like this."

"Not fast enough to draw any undue attention," Tavish reminded Levin.

"Not my first time doing shady shit." Levin slammed the lid of the trunk, locking them inside.

He probably deserved that, but he was on edge knowing Karolena was in enemy territory, no matter their precautions.

"Focus on your job," Jordan reminded Tavish through his comms.

Though it was too dark for their boss to see on the bodycam, Tavish nodded.

It probably wasn't more than ten minutes, but it felt as long as the entire flight before Levin's car slowed. Over the comms he heard the guard manning the gate welcome Levin home. If the guy noticed Karolena wasn't with Levin, he certainly didn't question his superior about it. The poor bastard did prepare to scan the car for bugs or bombs, neither of which would do.

So Levin barked at the man. "Do you want me to tell Vladimir I was late bringing him news of his wife because you held me up?"

"No, sir. Of course not."

Levin didn't bother with anything more and instead took off toward Vladimir's stronghold, assuming he was following the plan. They zipped along the winding drive Tavish had checked out on satellite imagery during their briefings before coming to a stop once more. They should have been in one of the five garages attached to the stone mansion, which appeared more like a fortress than a home.

Levin got out of the car, tapped on the trunk twice to let them know it was clear, then popped it open before disappearing inside ahead of them.

The plan was for him to run interference while Legend and Tavish crept up the rear staircase to Vladimir's personal suite. If he was there, fine. If not, they would wait for his return. Either way...this was going to be over soon.

Tavish drew his gun and flicked off the safety. He shared a knowing stare with Legend, proud and grateful to be doing this with the person who got him most in the world. He took a long deep breath, then a second before he put his hand on the doorknob and turned. After checking both ways down the hallway on the other side, he found it clear and sprinted up the staircase to the right. At the top, he counted doors.

One...two...three...*four.*

Tavish glanced at Legend, who gave the ready signal.

But something held him back. There was no one around and no commotion down below on Levin's return. Could this be a setup after all?

Was he about to open this door and be taken out as easily as he hoped to get rid of Vladimir?

"Second thoughts?" Jordan asked over the comms. Their boss would never push them to ignore their intuition. They'd all heard him tell the story about how his first partner had sensed the ambush they were about to walk into. The one where he'd died.

Tavish took a split second to weigh the situation. "Karolena trusts Levin and I trust her."

Legend nodded.

"Then get in there. And good luck." Jordan gave Tavish the push he needed to nudge open the door. The room they crept into, a living room, was dark but the one beyond it was bright. A light glowed from beneath the connecting door. That was Vladimir's bedroom, the cage Karolena had been confined to for so long.

As they inched toward the space, he heard grunting, then a thud followed by a wail. "Shut up and take it like Karolena does."

Tavish flew into a zone he hadn't experienced since the moment he realized that his entire family had been slaughtered by someone he'd thought he loved.

Pure rage caused him to morph into something less than human, entirely primal. This time he actually had an outlet for his fury. He hauled back and kicked the door in, rushing into the bedroom in time to rip Vladimir from the woman he was assaulting before he could do any more damage.

She scrambled backward, falling off the far side of the bed, and huddling in the corner where she promptly passed out. Good. They couldn't afford any witnesses.

"You keep Karolena's name out of your filthy mouth." Tavish struck the bastard across the face with his gun, knocking him to the ground on the other side of the bed from his most recent victim.

"Friends of my wife?" Vladimir acted like he couldn't feel the damage Tavish had done to his jaw, though his fingers pressed against the spot and came away bloody. "Interesting."

"She was never yours," Legend snarled, shocking Tavish. The other man had never lost his shit before even if his brand of anger was a calm collected rage.

"Take him out," Jordan ordered.

"Haven't you ever seen *Batman*?" It was well known James idolized Robin. "If you talk to the bad guy for too long, they get away."

True enough, but it was important to Tavish that Vladimir knew exactly which of his actions were coming back to haunt him in the final moments of his life.

"I see it took two men to replace me." His oily smirk only enraged Tavish more.

"No. She was always more than enough for any man, and especially for a monster like you," Tavish informed him. "This is for Karolena. And her mom. And that woman you just hurt. And all the others who wished you were dead. Now you are."

Vladimir lunged for them as if he refused to admit defeat.

Tavish fired his weapon. At such close range, there was no missing. But whether he killed Vladimir or Legend did, they'd never know since they pulled their triggers at the same time.

Despite their silencers, an alarm sounded. Jordan had passed along their progress to Levin and he'd initialized the next stage of their plan. The part where they instigated enough chaos that they were able to leverage it to get the fuck out of there.

"Where is Levin?" Legend asked command center.

"Incoming. Three seconds," Ruby responded.

The outer door opened then closed, Levin locking it behind him if all was going as planned. But instead of Levin, it was a more compact man with blond hair who rushed inside first. He took one look at them, their guns, and the mess they'd made of Vladimir before drawing up short.

He aimed his own weapon at them and Levin froze.

This was the part Tavish had hated the most about their plan. But when the man attempted to shoot him, his weapon didn't fire. Thankfully, Levin had somehow emptied it as he'd promised he would.

"Levin!" he called. And the guy materialized from the shadows.

"Kon." He wrapped his hand around his boyfriend's gun and pushed it down, aimed at the floor instead of Tavish. "We only have a second."

Though Levin switched to Russian, the Shields' tech translated for them into their earpieces.

"You did this? You're responsible?" Konstantin's pretty eyes went wide. "They're going to kill you."

"No," Tavish spoke up. "*We're* responsible for this."

"He's going to lead the organization in an attempt to find poor Vlad's killer. And you're coming with us." Legend took a hood and a couple of oversized zip ties from his cargo pants. "A hostage always comes in handy when making our exit."

Konstantin ignored Legend and whipped his stare to Levin.

"I love you." Levin didn't waste a single precious moment. He grabbed Konstantin's face and kissed him as if it was the last time. Because it might have been. "And that's why you have to go."

"What?" Konstantin's face reflected an emotion Tavish knew all too well. Betrayal. Anger followed quickly on its heels. "What the hell is going on?"

"This is going to get ugly. I'm willing to gamble myself, but not you." Levin pointed him toward Legend and shoved his shoulders. "What they'll do to me if they catch me is bad, but it would be a hundred times worse if they so much as put a bruise on you."

"I have no idea what you've gotten yourself into, but I'd rather die than leave you to deal with it on your own." Konstantin stood his ground despite Legend strapping his hands behind his back.

"Time to go, boys." Jordan's tone allowed no room for argument.

"I couldn't live with that." Levin shot Tavish a look so powerful it nearly knocked him over. "Remember, not one hair on his head out of place or I'll cut your balls clean off."

Tavish nodded. He owed Levin this. After all, he'd done the same for Karolena. "Good luck."

To his credit, Konstantin didn't fight. He accepted that the one man who could have changed his fate had decided not to. He hung like deadweight over Legend's shoulder as they climbed out the window.

The Heat would have been impressed by the fireman's lift he used when they scurried down the ladder Levin had placed there while they were taking care of Vladimir. They dashed into the garage, stuffed Konstantin into the backseat of the car, jumped into the front themselves, and took off.

They didn't even slow as they approached the gate, relying on Levin to keep his end of the bargain. And as they approached, it swung open, giving them barely enough clearance to rocket through before shutting and locking behind them.

Though it took a few minutes longer, they followed a circuitous route back to the jet. On the dark roads on the outskirts of the city, it would have been easy to spot the headlights of anyone giving chase.

When they were satisfied they were clear, they raced to the private airstrip, ditched the car by the side of the runway, and hauled their unconventional baggage onto the jet with them.

As Legend set Konstantin on one of the leather couches as gently as he could, given the man's thrashing, Tavish's stare locked with Karolena's.

She'd seen for herself that they would kill for her.

And that her personal hell had been destroyed.

Karolena was free. She no longer needed to run, or to hide. But she'd also seen that they could be merciless too. And he hoped she'd choose to stay with them anyway.

19

Aven fanned herself as her mind replayed on loop the kiss Levin had given Konstantin before banishing him from his inherited evil empire. After being surrounded by blissful trios every damn day, she'd thought she was immune to smoking hot public displays of affection, but apparently not so much.

It could have been the angst of not knowing when, or if, Levin would see his lover ever again that took it to the next level. She suspected it had more to do with the people themselves, though.

Which made her the world's biggest dumbass.

They were clearly obsessed with each other. How they'd hidden their bond, or their queerness, from the mafia this long was a mystery to her. They must have been incredible actors in addition to smoking hot and—in Levin's case—borderline assholes with confidence that edged into arrogance.

What did it say that his attitude had turned her on from the moment he strode into their midst like he didn't give a single fuck about the collection of weapons pointed in his direction?

More fanning. Faster fanning.

It didn't hurt that he made some mean Russian pancakes. They'd spent an hour or two together in the middle of the night, while taking a refueling break during their intel gathering. When she'd offered to heat up leftover pizza, he'd insisted on whipping up a batch of *syrnikis*, topping them with fresh fruit.

Something about the very idea of a mafia kingpin slinging batter in an apron, taking care of her when his entire existence was about to be thrust into chaos, had grabbed her attention and not let go ever since. Which was a problem considering he'd spent most of that time gushing about his boyfriend and insisting she promise to take care of the man, who probably could handle himself just fine if the glimpse she'd had from Tavish's bodycam was any indication.

"They're here," Nolan called from outside the jet. He, Marcus, and Knox surrounded the approaching car to verify everything checked before allowing it too close to the plane.

Aven leaned up against the open door of her cockpit as Legend hauled a compact—though very fit—man onboard her jet, his arms bound behind his back. "I hope we're not going to have to leave him like that for the entire flight."

She didn't relish the idea of his discomfort, especially not after the especially rude ending to his evening.

Tavish deferred to Aven. "You make the call. You're the one who has to work the next twelve hours and I don't want to do anything that's going to make you uncomfortable or put us in a pinch."

Aven shrugged. "Let's talk to him first, then decide."

"Just because you put this damn hood over my face doesn't mean I can't hear you." Konstantin proved he had no shortage of sass. She agreed with Levin's assessment from headquarters. There was something about him that reminded her of James.

From the other line of their reopened comms, their office manager giggled. "I like him already."

Trouble was, so did Aven. And she didn't want to let that cloud her judgement when everyone onboard relied on her, literally putting their lives in her hands on every mission.

"Take that off him." Aven pointed at his hood. It had mostly been for show anyway, so that the guards and any security footage wouldn't suggest he'd been sent away and instead anyone looking would assume he'd been stolen.

When Legend removed it, Konstantin shot daggers at them. She was glad they'd searched him thoroughly for weapons before bringing him onboard. "I can assure you I'm going to be a giant pain in your ass. So you might as well toss me out before you get going, wherever the fuck it is you're headed."

"No can do." Tavish shook his head.

From where she'd lurked behind the agents, whether because she was nervous to interact with someone from her old life, or because she'd been laser focused on following Tavish and Legend's order to keep her ass on the plane and out of the way, Karolena spoke up. "We promised Levin we'd take care of you."

"Karolena!" He sat up straighter when he caught sight of the gorgeous blonde. "Holy shit. No offense, but I assumed you were dead."

"Reasonable." She shook her head. "But no, Levin smuggled me out. And now he's doing the same for you."

"I won't leave him." He got to his feet, but Legend put his massive hand on Konstantin's shoulder and smushed him back down.

"You don't have a choice. I'm sorry," Aven told him as kindly as she could. "In fact, Nolan, get the doors."

"No!" Konstantin struggled, but with his arms still fettered and Legend towering over him, it was pointless.

When they'd locked themselves in, Konstantin sagged.

Karolena approached him and crouched by his knee. She put her hand on his leg. "These people are part of a team called Shields. They're sort of assassins, but they only kill bad guys."

"I noticed." Right. It wouldn't be news to Konstantin, given the state of Vladimir's skull. "How do you know we're not next?"

"Because they're helping me make my escape permanent. And Levin too. He's going to bring the whole thing down, just watch." She really seemed to believe what she was saying. "And because..."

Tavish edged closer to her and so did Legend.

"Wow. You move fast." Konstantin was very in tune with the emotional undercurrents running between them. Though honestly it was pretty obvious now that they weren't hiding the possessive heat they shared.

Karolena looked away and blushed.

Fuck that. Aven would have said so but she didn't want to interrupt.

Konstantin redeemed himself when he added, "I'm not judging, Karolena. Lord knows you earned the right to be happy and sleep with whoever the hell you want after surviving Vladimir. I'm just a little...surprised."

"Me too." She held out her hands so that Tavish took one and Legend the other. There could be no doubt she was with them both. Not only for a fling, but for something lasting.

Motherfucker. Aven grumbled to herself. She'd seen this happen often enough that she knew what she was looking at. And yet again, it wasn't her in the middle of a hot guy sandwich.

"But Levin..." Konstantin couldn't be distracted for long. "Are they helping him? He doesn't stand a chance on his own."

Aven spoke up then. "We are. He wanted you to know that he has a plan and that he fully intends to come for you as soon as his work here is finished."

"The man has an ego the size of this jet." Konstantin rolled his eyes. "Sure, he mostly deserves it, but if he's trading my life for his, it's pointless. I'd never be able to live with that."

"I promise you they're supporting his efforts." Karolena looked to Aven. "Can we untie him?"

"Are you going to behave yourself for the flight?" Aven arched a brow.

"Might as well. Need to survive to chew Levin's ass out later." Konstantin turned his head to stare out the window.

She could have sworn she heard Nolan crack a joke about how much Levin would like that, but she was focused on what she needed to do to get them in the air.

"Let him loose," Aven told Legend, then made final preparations for takeoff. When she was about to head into the cockpit, she turned to Konstantin one last time and said, "I'm sorry your boyfriend is so damn cocky."

"You and me both." A hint of a smile flicked over his lips as he shot her a rueful glance.

"But it really is for your own benefit." Aven turned and raised her voice so they could hear her as she took her place. "Everyone strap in. We'll be up in a couple minutes."

As she went through her routine, she heard Karolena continue to reassure Konstantin. "Would it be okay if I gave you a hug? I remember what it was like when I did this, not so long ago. I'm sure you're in shock."

"Yeah. Thanks."

It was quiet for a while then Karolena told him, "You're going to like it at Shields. It's nothing like this place. It feels like an entirely different planet without judgement or fear."

Konstantin's *humpf* didn't hold a lot of conviction, but Aven made it her personal mission to change his mind in the coming weeks.

"Would you like some water or something to eat?" Karolena asked him.

"I think I'd mostly like some time to think. This is a lot." Konstantin sounded tired. Aven was sure he'd be out not long after they reached altitude. It happened a lot when she picked up the agents and their adrenaline crashed.

Well, either that or...

Sure enough, Karolena, Legend, and Tavish angled toward each other. Aven turned around long enough to witness them wrapped together in a three-way hug. "Thank God you made it out safe."

"Of course we did. We had you waiting to come back to." Legend kissed Karolena and she didn't even flinch despite Konstantin observing as Legend passed her to Tavish to do the same.

"Is it okay if we go talk in private?" Karolena asked her men, edging toward the bedroom at the back of the plane.

"I swear this jet sees more action than a window in the red light district." Knox chuckled. "Don't forget there are more of us here who'd like to 'take a nap' on the way home."

Konstantin's eyes got bigger as he looked between Kennedy, Marcus, and Knox. Aven barely picked up his whispered, "Damn. What have I gotten into?"

It had her smiling to herself as she flipped on the engines.

Tavish surprised her then by declaring, "This is about more than sex. At least for me, and hopefully for them too."

Of course they'd all known it was, but they hadn't expected him to admit it to himself, never mind so publicly.

Legend responded hesitantly, "I would never try to claim either of you..."

"Well, I'm claiming you both," Karolena interrupted, flinging her arms around their necks and hugging them to her.

"Me too." Tavish kissed each of them.

"That's precious, now sit your asses down and put your seatbelts on until I tell you you're clear to go to the bedroom and take your turn tearing up the mattress." Aven got serious when she was ready to fly.

Nolan roared with laughter while Konstantin simply stared at them all like he'd entered an alternate universe. She figured that for him, it sort of was. Hell, it was for her too.

Aven tried not to let her envy sneak through her overwhelming happiness for her friends, but during the long hours on their way home, it was hard not to wonder if it would ever be her turn. She cleared her mind of everything but gauges and lights and a panoramic view of the world passing below.

But even the amber glow of one of her controls reminded her of staring into Levin's golden eyes before he charged down the plane stairs to do what he had to in order to set things to rights. She could respect his decision, even if she was afraid it would end badly.

How would it feel if a man like him had that kind of fierce dedication to her?

She desperately wanted to find out.

Someday.

Aven couldn't help but imagine Levin getting smaller and smaller in the distance, unsure of why that thought unsettled her so much. So she concentrated on doing what she'd promised him—swooping through the night at hundreds of miles per hour to deliver his most precious cargo to the safety of Shields until he could reclaim his man.

At least she'd get to see him again when he did.

For Aven, Levin, and Konstantin's story, read SHARED

"Jayne is the queen of multipartner romance!"
SHARED
Powertools: The Shields
NEW YORK TIMES & USA TODAY BESTSELLING AUTHOR
JAYNE RYLON

If you'd like to start at the very beginning with the Powertools Crew, you can download a discounted boxset of the first six books HERE.

Yes, I know it says complete series but I wrote a seventh book more recently and haven't gotten around to updating the boxset yet, sorry!

You can find the seventh Powertools book, More the Merrier, HERE.

They are also featured in four books in the Powertools: The Original Crew Returns series starting with Screwed HERE

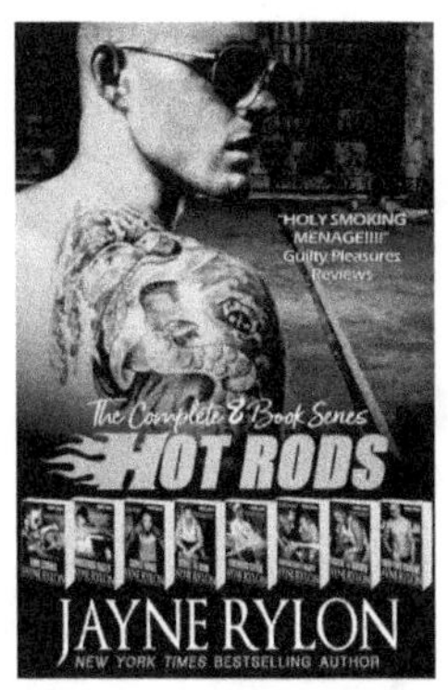

If you missed out on the Powertools: Hot Rods series, you can buy all eight books in a discounted single-volume boxset by clicking HERE.

To read more about the Hot Rides gang, start with Quinn, Trevon, and Devra's story, Wild Ride, click HERE.

Did you know Jayne brought the original Powertools crew back for four more books? Click HERE to get caught up.

CLAIM A $5 GIFT CERTIFICATE

Jayne is so sure you will love her books, she'd like you to try any one of your choosing for free. Claim your $5 gift certificate by signing up for her newsletter. You'll also learn about freebies, new releases, extras, appearances, and more!

www.jaynerylon.com/newsletter

WHAT WAS YOUR FAVORITE PART?

Did you enjoy this book? If so, please leave a review and tell your friends about it. Word of mouth and online reviews are immensely helpful and greatly appreciated.

JAYNE'S SHOP

Check out Jayne's online shop for autographed print books, direct download ebooks, reading-themed apparel up to size 5XL, mugs, tote bags, notebooks, Mr. Rylon's wood (you'll have to see it for yourself!) and more.
www.jaynerylon.com/shop

LISTEN UP!

The majority of Jayne's books are also available in audio format on Audible, Amazon and iTunes.

ABOUT THE AUTHOR

Jayne Rylon is a New York Times and USA Today bestselling author, who has sold more than two million copies of her books. She has received numerous industry awards including the Romantic Times Reviewers' Choice Award for Best Indie Erotic Romance and the Swirl Award, which recognizes excellence in diverse romance. She is an Honor Roll member of the Romance Writers of America. Her stories used to begin as daydreams in seemingly endless business meetings, but now she is a full time author, who employs the skills she learned from her straight-laced corporate existence in the business of writing. She lives in Ohio with her husband, the infamous Mr. Rylon, and kittens they foster for a rescue organization. When she can escape her purple office, she loves to travel the world, avoid speeding tickets in her beloved Sky, SCUBA dive, and–of course–read.

Jayne Loves To Hear From Readers
www.jaynerylon.com
contact@jaynerylon.com
PO Box 10, Pickerington, OH 43147

facebook.com/jaynerylon

twitter.com/JayneRylon

instagram.com/jaynerylon

youtube.com/jaynerylonbooks

bookbub.com/profile/jayne-rylon

amazon.com/author/jaynerylon

ALSO BY JAYNE RYLON

4-EVER

A New Adult Reverse Harem Series

4-Ever Theirs

4-Ever Mine

EVER AFTER DUET

Reverse Harem Featuring Characters From The 4-Ever Series

Fourplay

Fourkeeps

EVER & ALWAYS DUET

Reverse Harem Featuring Characters from the 4-Ever and Ever After Duets

Four Money

Four Love

POWERTOOLS: THE ORIGINAL CREW

Five Guys Who Get It On With Each Other & One Girl. Enough Said?

Kate's Crew

Morgan's Surprise

Kayla's Gift

Devon's Pair

Nailed to the Wall

Hammer it Home

More the Merrier *NEW*

POWERTOOLS: HOT RODS

Powertools Spin Off. Keep up with the Crew plus...

Seven Guys & One Girl. Enough Said?

King Cobra

Mustang Sally

Super Nova

Rebel on the Run

Swinger Style

Barracuda's Heart

Touch of Amber

Long Time Coming

POWERTOOLS: HOT RIDES

Powertools and Hot Rods Spin Off.

Menage and Motorcycles

Wild Ride

Slow Ride

Hard Ride

Joy Ride

Rough Ride

POWERTOOLS: RETURN OF THE CREW

The original crew is back with more steamy menage stories!

Screwed

Drilled

Grind

Pound

POWERTOOLS: THE SHIELDS

Do-gooder Polyamorous Assassins in MMF Menages

Found

Lost

Brazen

Broken

Claimed

Shared

MEN IN BLUE

Hot Cops Save Women In Danger

Night is Darkest

Razor's Edge

Mistress's Master

Spread Your Wings

Wounded Hearts

Bound For You

DIVEMASTERS

Sexy SCUBA Instructors By Day, Doms On A Mega-Yacht By Night

Going Down

Going Deep

Going Hard

STANDALONE

Menage

Middleman

Nice & Naughty

Contemporary

Where There's Smoke

Report For Booty

COMPASS BROTHERS

Modern Western Family Drama Plus Lots Of Steamy Sex

Northern Exposure

Southern Comfort

Eastern Ambitions

Western Ties

COMPASS GIRLS

Daughters Of The Compass Brothers Drive Their Dads Crazy And Fall In Love

Winter's Thaw

Hope Springs

Summer Fling

Falling Softly

COMPASS BOYS

Sons Of The Compass Brothers Fall In Love

Heaven on Earth

Into the Fire

Still Waters

Light as Air

PLAY DOCTOR

Naughty Sexual Psychology Experiments Anyone?

Dream Machine

Healing Touch

RED LIGHT

A Hooker Who Loves Her Job

Complete Red Light Series Boxset

FREE - Through My Window - FREE

Star

Can't Buy Love

Free For All

PICK YOUR PLEASURES

Choose Your Own Adventure Romances!

Pick Your Pleasure

Pick Your Pleasure 2

RACING FOR LOVE

MMF Menages With Race-Car Driver Heroes

Complete Series Boxset

Driven

Shifting Gears

PARANORMALS

Vampires, Witches, And A Man Trapped In A Painting

Paranormal Double Pack Boxset

Picture Perfect

Reborn

PENTHOUSE PLEASURES

Naughty Manhattanite Neighbors Find Kinky Love

Taboo

Kinky

Sinner

Mentor

ROAMING WITH THE RYLONS

Non-fiction Travelogues about Jayne & Mr. Rylon's Adventures

Australia and New Zealand